A SPARROW HAS WINGS

JOHN W. GIBSON

12/4/14

To Keith

Put Wings to your dreams

John W. Gibson

HALF MOON
PUBLISHERS

First published by Half Moon Publishers 02/01/05

ISBN: 0-615-12798-3

This book is printed on acid free paper.

DEDICATION

The Tuskegee Airmen; that proud, courageous, group of young African American men who during WWII dared to defy skeptics and racists to complete the rigorous training program at Tuskegee, Alabama and become a heroic group of fighter pilots.

I specifically want to thank George "Spanky" Roberts, Herman "Ace" Lawson and John "Mr. Death" Whitehead who, along with their wives, shared their story with me.

ACKNOWLEDGEMENTS

Janice Yvonne Hecht
Stephan (Steve) G. Gibson
Howard W. Hecht
Pearl Lawson
Edith Roberts
Vava M. Bowers
Henrietta H Gibson
Liza Gibson
Kate Kelton
Patsy Murray
Shirley Ingram
Shallie Bey
Ivan Diggs
Rev. James Jenkins
Karen Ewing-Harper
Tom Pope
Paul Burt
Gary R. Brunson (Cover Painting & Design)
Min Gates
Richard Eisleben
Eugene W. Jackson III
Ron & Rose Scroggins
Janet Sue Gibson
Lucille Martindale
Joseph D. Caver
Paul Bodley
William "Bill" Bell
Tuskegee Library – Tuskegee, Alabama
Research Agency Maxwell AFB – Alabama

CHAPTER ONE

Jordan Wingate strolled confidently toward the tiny prop plane painted with *Greer's Flyers* in bold red letters on the side. He was fully aware of the doubts the majority of Americans had regarding the Negro's ability to fly. The doubts among inhabitants of Columbus, Ohio, were no less strong or pervasive. The cool look on his dark, normally expressive face masked his slight tremble of nervousness. Chewing gum usually calmed him at times like this. His mother Sarah, small and frail, straining on tiptoes to see over the crowd in front of her, knew that his chewing gum was a sign of nervousness. His father, Mose, who was no doubt teasing her about her height disadvantage, also knew about Jordan's habit of chewing gum to calm his nerves. And Jordan knew that the two of them were nervous for him. Besides that, he did not have any chewing gum. "When was the last time I forgot?" he thought. He couldn't remember the last time he did not have a stick of spearmint or Beechnut tucked in a jacket or pants pocket. Using his next best remedy, he hummed a few bars of *"My Blue Heaven."*

The closer he drew to the plane the more animated became the growing crowd. The people were filling the bleachers to cheer on the acrobatic exploits of the participants of the Third Annual Colored Air and Ground Show.

Jordan's ultimate goal was to be accepted by the U.S. Army Air Corps. The cause of his uneasiness stemmed from factors other than the attitudes of white America toward Negroes flying. He could not count the times a friend or relative questioned his sanity. How many times had someone said, "You know, if God wanted you to fly, don't you think He'd have given you some wings?" Or, someone said, "I know it's rough down here, but at least I've got some ground under my feet." Jordan had long ago stopped pointing out to people the

1

statistics showing how many more of them died in automobile accidents than in plane crashes. Or, for that matter, how many more died in accidents in the home. The questions, combined with the unyielding attitudes of Americans, presented a new seemingly insurmountable obstacle. He even knew of a few friends who had given up their quest in the face of obstacles. He had to admit that even he, "Mr. Eternal Optimist," had to struggle with doubt a time or two. He had to look in the mirror and ask himself whether he honestly thought that he would ever become a fighter pilot protecting America from a near inevitable confrontation with Adolf Hitler's Luftwaffe. Then he thought of Hitler's attitude toward Jesse Owens during the 1936 Olympics, and toward his idol, Joe "Brown Bomber" Louis, during his fights against Max Schmeling. Hitler considered them, as he did all Negroes, as inferior and less than human. Those thoughts always served to renew his determination, to stoke his coals, to charge his batteries.

Excitement raced through his total being as he climbed into the cockpit, a rather tight fit for the 165 pounds that were spread evenly over his 5-feet 11-inch frame. He checked the instrument panel thoroughly. After starting the engine and before opening the throttle, he made sure that all of the gauges on the panel were in the green. Relieved to see that everything was working, he opened the throttle and began to taxi toward the runway.

The spectators rose as one and began to cheer and clap. He recalled his days as a running back on the high school and college football teams. The excitement he had felt when running past frustrated would-be tacklers was the same kind of excitement he felt now. "You ain't seen nothing yet," he murmured.

All eyes were fastened on him. Children who had been rollicking under and through the bleachers now gave him their rapt attention. Young women who had been chatting were standing, screaming, and pretending to swoon and faint. He could see Mose, wide and towering over everyone, clapping. And he knew that his mother, hidden behind the crowd, was doing the same. He also knew that she would be praying fervently from the moment he left the ground until he landed. The atmosphere was extremely festive. A slight breeze stirred the pennants and flags. One teenager pounded a drum, one blew a saxophone, and two blew trumpets, adding to the ear-splitting shouts of the crowd. His adrenaline increased when he opened the throttle wider. The roar of the motor drowned out the crowd noise and he focused his attention on pulling the stick back gradually as the plane lifted smoothly off the runway.

The air was free of turbulence and the clouds were high. He flew away from the crowd until he reached 2,000 feet. Then he went into a turn, banking the plane skillfully as if he had been flying forever. After moving into sight of his audience, he thought, "I can't let them leave here without being dazzled." After all, there were news reporters down there. They had become more visible after rumors abounded that the War Department would admit Negroes into the Army Air Corps. *Who knows? Might be a military bigwig down there. Got to give them a closer look at Jordan Wingate in control of this bird.* He dove to within 1500 feet of the crowd in the bleachers, sending them into a more celebratory display of standing, waving, screeching. "That ought to open their eyes," he whispered. The thought of the probability of his mother's hysterics was sobering. But he had to perform once more before landing. He banked the plane and headed toward the crowd again. This time he dove even closer forcing a few of those who were standing to scurry in mock fright.

Not until he had touched down and guided the plane to a bumpy landing did he experience a coldness inside and uneven breathing. He looked up and whispered a quick "thanks" before climbing out of the cockpit and calmly removing his headgear and goggles. As he strolled nonchalantly toward his destination, the crowd gave him a thunderous reception in appreciation of his calm response to a dangerous situation.

By the time he reached Velma Greer, the diminutive owner of the flying school, who stood talking with two reporters, he had shaken hands with several men, been hugged by countless young women and tugged at by several boys, one of whom he was now carrying. The crowd cheered so robustly and continuously that he was finding it difficult to remember he was mortal and that he had come but part way in his quest for uniqueness. He had decided that his mother and father had not been able to get through the crowd when he spotted them. He stopped shaking hands with his admirers long enough to embrace them.

"I had to wake your mama out of a dead faint," big Mose said. "That's why you're just now seeing us." His wide smile revealed a gold tooth that gleamed in the sun.

"Listen who's talking," Sarah countered, gently touching him. "We're real proud of you, son."

Jordan kissed her and shook Mose's hand. The latter pulled him into a strong hug.

Velma Greer introduced him to a reporter from the local Negro newspaper. The reporter was young and eager to do his job.

"Mr. Wingate," he said, "you gave us quite a scare for a short time."

A crowd of Jordan's friends had gathered around him.

"I was feeling a little scared myself," he admitted.

Velma Greer laughed. "Don't let Mr. Wingate fool you. He doesn't think he's flying unless he attempts some crazy acrobatic stunt."

Jordan laughed. "Ma'am, you're not saying that I planned that?"

"Just call him Jordan "Showboat" Wingate," a friend said.

"One thing you'll have to admit is that he can fly," Velma said. "And he's only had a couple lessons." She turned to the reporter. "I think you'd have to write that he's a born flier. A natural."

The reporter checked through his notes. He nodded at Jordan and added a few more lines. "I understand a Mr. White and ah---"

"Spencer," Velma offered. "Dale and Chauncy, two of more than a hundred Negro pilots with licenses."

"That's right. I heard that two years ago they flew from Chicago to Washington, D.C."

Velma laughed. "In the most antiquated excuse for a plane there ever was. Looked like it was stuck together with Scotch tape and gum."

Velma Greer was not only beautiful, but also witty, feisty, and tough. She had a coffee-colored complexion and a combination of female softness and male toughness that enhanced her attractiveness with women, most of whom did not have what it took to enter the world of aviation, much less run a flight school. Her toughness and tendency toward boldness made her more acceptable to pilots, mechanics and other men in an industry that was still in its infancy.

The reporter directed the photographer to shoot a few shots of Jordan standing next to the plane. He said, "You'd think that Mr. White's and Mr. Spencer's achievements were proof enough that we can fly." He motioned for Jordan to act as if he were climbing into the cockpit to prepare for takeoff.

"They did convince one of the wheels in D.C." Velma said. "Senator Harry Truman. I heard that he really admired their courage."

"Who knows how many more of us there are with that same courage?" The reporter motioned to the photographer that they had taken enough pictures. "In spite of what the War Department says."

"I just hope they pass that bill to let us into the Army Air Corps soon," Jordan said.

"They did. Earlier today," Velma assured him.

The reporter nodded in agreement.

"Good," Jordan said, trying to contain the thrill her announcement sparked within him. "Now if they put it into practice."

"Well, that might be easier said than done." The reporter was concerned about the photographer leaving him behind. "Just because a law was passed doesn't necessarily mean there won't continue to be major opposition to its being practiced."

"The NAACP," Velma reminded them. "Don't underestimate them."

In his office in Washington, D.C. Colonel Buford Saunders, a huge red-faced Southerner, glowered at an article in the morning newspaper. What the article said, "Bill Passed to Train Negro Fighter Pilots," was anathema to him. If there was one thing he was sure of, it was that the War Department was making a terrible mistake. "Damn Yankee know-it-alls," he said. He lit one of his favorite cigars, then struggled out of a chair that had been designed for a smaller body. He paced around his spacious office, trying to calm down. As if to verify what a military man should look like, he paused to emulate the pose of a painting of himself that occupied an entire wall. The painting was of a trimmer and much younger Buford Saunders, as arrogant then as he was now. He straightened his shoulders and thrust out his chest. He could hold the pose only moments before he was out of breath. No matter. Sticking the cigar in his mouth, he crossed his arms over his chest. Now he was once again the heroic leader returning from Europe after World War I.

The phone rang, startling him back into the present. The few steps across the room to pick up the receiver had him wheezing. "'Lo, Glenn," he said. "What in hell is it coming to? Since when did we start questioning whether 'Nigras' could fly? Hell, we spend one hell of a time just teaching them to march!" He laughed at Glenn Morley's response. "Well I sure don't care what the Senator from New York says. By the time one of them learned how to figure out an instrument panel the war'd be over!" So Morley, the Secretary of War, didn't totally agree with him. What did a spoiled intellectual from the North know? He was on a roll. "Fighter pilots? I don't care what the damned NAACP wants! I say 'Nigras' can't fly!" He slammed the phone into the receiver.

Jordan arose early in the morning with a feeling of expectation. This would be a special day, something more than a typical dreary winter day in Flytown when the cold wind whipped off the Olentangy River, causing him to question why he lived there during this time of the year. As soon as he was out of bed, he turned the radio dial searching for some news. After dressing for his workday as a youth counselor at the Godman Guild, he retrieved the newspaper. Nothing.

However, he was not the least bit surprised when a fellow counselor informed him that there had been an announcement on the radio that would interest him. Apparently President Roosevelt had signed a bill to admit Negroes into the Army Air Corps. At long last he would have his chance to do something great.

At home, he met the iceman making his daily delivery. Although Jordan was wearing a white shirt, he carried the fifty-pound block of ice into the house and lifted it effortlessly into the icebox.

Mose looked up from an ear of corn he was shucking. "What'd you do, lock up the guild early?"

"No, sir. They let me go early. I was too excited to stay." He wiped his hands on the towel his mother handed him. "Heard about this on the radio." He reached into his briefcase and placed a copy of the *Columbus Dispatch* on the table. "It's official, Mom, Daddy." The headline read, "Army Air Corps To Accept Negroes."

His father and mother looked at each other and at him.

"Son," Mose said, a look of skepticism on his face. "How long have we heard this was supposed to happen?"

"Well, now it has, Daddy. The president came through."

Sarah put on her glasses and scanned the article and then she removed them and touched Jordan's hand. There was a faraway expression in her eyes. "A long time ago your daddy dreamed of being a doctor, but he couldn't go to college." Her expression of tenderness deepened as she looked at him. "After that I guess he took to drinking anything that had alcohol in it."

Mose said just above a whisper, but with a firmness with which Jordan was all too familiar. "We sure don't need another falling down drunk in the Wingate family." Then followed a moment of silence in which more and more lately he was able to bring about a few words of prayer during times like this.

Annie, Jordan's young sister, entered. Despite her youth, she was on her way to matching Mose in size. "Daddy," she said playfully, "You didn't need to worry about either of us drinking too much whiskey. You didn't leave very much."

"Never mind," Sarah said. "Son, counseling brings in a good steady pay. Any girl would be happy to have a husband making the kind of money you make."

"Sure, but think how happy one would be if they had a husband flying for Uncle Sam," Jordan said. "Hey, Mama, this talk about marrying is a little bit too serious for me."

Annie scanned the newspaper article. "Big brother, are you sure this ain't something else for you to grow bored with and quit?"

Jordan grabbed her in a bear hug.

"Fly?" Mose said. "Boy, you used to get real sick when somebody even suggested that you climb a tree. How you gonna go way up there in an airplane?"

The others agreed.

"That was then," Jordan said, in a tone as firm as that of Mose's, "this is now."

In the silence that filled the room Sarah crossed over and looked into the oven to check on the apple pie she was baking. The strong scent of apples and cinnamon pervaded the kitchen.

"Dreaming anyhow," Mose said in a hushed tone of voice. "By the time Uncle Sam starts trusting Negroes with airplanes I'll be dead and buried... and so will you."

Everyone but Jordan laughed nervously.

Sarah, her eyes filled with pride behind tears, touched him. "I guess one of my children had to be a dreamer like his daddy used to be."

Mose nodded. Jordan could see that he was not thoroughly convinced that Uncle Sam really meant to follow through on his promise. But the article and the news on the radio was all that he needed to start reaching for his dream.

That night Jordan worked on a letter to be sent to his congressman. Three hours later he was satisfied that it said enough about his credentials for acceptance into the Army Air Corps. He hoped that it conveyed his enthusiasm. He knew about the civilian flight-training program that was available at a small number of Negro colleges. Velma Greer's flight school came under a different executive order and was the only school available to young Negroes. He had no idea how many Negroes throughout the United States were as anxious as he was to join.

During the day, he had thought of something else that might help his cause. He arrived at the flight school just as Velma was about to close shop for the day.

"I need your endorsement on this letter to my congressman," he said.

"All right, Hotshot," she said with a mischievous twinkle in her eyes. "But first you're going to have to log some more flight hours. This time without me assisting you."

They broke into laughter.

"Jordan Wingate, if you can't fly one of those fighter planes, I don't know who can."

They revised the letter and mailed it that night. Now all he had to do was endure the wait for the response. He also had to endure the continued skepticism of friends and relatives. Each morning when he arrived at the Godman Guild until he left each afternoon, he heard comments ranging from "Uncle Sam will probably wait until you get fed up with waiting and decide to say to hell with it" to "The qualifications will probably be too tough for you to meet." The majority of people with whom he talked thought the whole thing was a hoax, a cruel April Fool's joke in the middle of winter. Jordan listened, laughed, argued a bit, and maintained his confidence that he would be an ace fighter pilot. He would challenge Hitler's contention that blacks are inferior, and like the Brown Bomber and Jesse Owens, he would prove the Nazi leader wrong.

CHAPTER TWO

Colonel Buford Saunders was not a man given to quick change in his way of thinking. From the time he was one of two young sons of the owner of a huge cotton gin in Mississippi, he had manifested the trait of stubborn inflexibility. He set his mind to achieving something and did not let up until he had either succeeded or failed to do so. So strong was his determination that the failures were few. The same determination that had propelled him through high school and led him to become, at age eighteen, the manager at the cotton gin, had also enabled him to reach his current rank. That determination helped him to garner promotions without a college degree. His achievement added support to his long held philosophy that the importance placed on getting college degrees was blown way out of proportion. Buford earned his promotions through his achievements in World War I, through years of exemplary soldiering, through knowing the right people, and through a great amount of luck. But his stubbornness had always been his most prominent trait.

Now he faced a dilemma. In spite of what he knew about Negroes, he was being told that the War Department was going to accept them, and, of all things, teach them how to fly in combat. He approached the Secretary of War's office with ambivalent feelings. He would have much rather spent the first real spring day in Washington, D.C. meeting with the staff in the conference room next to his office. Instead, he had to spend time listening to Glenn Morley talk on and on about God knows what. It was simply another opportunity for Morley to display his intelligence about the United States' involvement in the European Theater. What in the hell did Morley know about war?

Inside Morley's office, Buford found the short,

bespectacled man in his usual jovial mood. He accepted his offer to sit and have a cup of coffee.

"Good to see you, Buford." Morley paused, smiled, and drummed his fingers on his desktop. "I've been racking my brain trying to come up with the man most, ah, most deserving the honor of commanding the new outfit at Tuskegee." He drummed his fingers some more. "You know, colored fighter pilots."

"Well sir, we did talk about several men we thought just might do a good job," Buford reminded him.

"I know we did," Morley whined. "Those might be good prospects, but I happen to think there's nobody more qualified or more deserving than the most esteemed colonel I know."

Buford was not one hundred percent sure that Morley meant him, yet was afraid to ask lest he find out. By the time he recovered enough to offer any complaints, Morley was accepting an important call from the President. "Excuse me, Buford," he said as he held his hand over the receiver, "your orders are being cut."

Buford seethed as he noticed the famous twinkle in Morley's eyes. Cursing in his mind and under his breath, he headed for his favorite tavern. The only way he could possibly survive this thunderbolt was to get totally drunk.

The next day he had his secretary contact Captain George Adams.

"Hard Rock," he said when the ex-ace pilot answered. "You've heard or read the nonsense about 'Nigras' being trained as fighter pilots? As usual, these damned fools have let their education get in the way of sense. Hell, if they can locate two of them with brains enough to learn to fly I'll be shocked… That's right. Not only has there never been any, but they don't have brains enough to ever master all of those controls." He laughed nearly uncontrollably. "Listen, old buddy, I've got a little favor

12

to ask. If I remember right, you do owe me one. I want you to use your contacts to find out if there are any of them that might have the smallest chance of qualifying."

In Atlanta, Georgia, Hollis Boyd hustled into a ballroom. Unlike most Negroes, he had just about everything going for him. He was twenty-six and highly educated. Not only was he the son of one of the Negro community's most distinguished doctors and one of its most qualified teachers, but his career as a lawyer had begun to flourish. Those who thought they knew him said that he was lucky, that everything he touched turned to gold and every decision he made was the right one. He truly had the Midas touch, but the few who really knew him knew that any success he had was a result of hard work. When he was young, he had learned from his father the value of keeping his nose to the grindstone. His father, an advocate of sticking with everything one undertook until it was finished, had been the number one role model for Hollis all of his young life.

Inside, Hollis brushed the rain off his suit coat and wiped it from his face with a handkerchief. Fortunately, it was just a drizzle. Neat was Hollis' favorite way of appearing. The room contained a combination of the sounds of a small band playing swing music and voices speaking softly and loudly. The mood was one of joviality and of celebration as Hollis wove his way through couples dancing. The dancers consisted of the Negro elite class. Light complexioned doctors, lawyers and other professionals swung their partners with varying intensity and dexterity to the strains of a Fats Waller tune. As Hollis moved forward, he spoke to those that he knew. Those that he did not know spoke to him. The women dressed in their finest gowns, furs, jewelry, and shoes were all beautiful.

13

He was excited by the turnout, and in turn was flattered and embarrassed by the looks that some of the females gave him even as they embarrassed their partners. Overhead, stretching across the front of the room was a colorful banner containing the words "GIVE THEM HELL, HOLLIS."

Almost directly under the banner he spotted his father. At nearly the same time his father spotted him and moved toward him.

"Friends!" boomed Charles Boyd, a man with a neatly trimmed mustache sprinkled with gray. "I invited you here to honor one of the first Negroes selected to fly in the Army Air Corps!" His voice had a melodious tone and carried enough power to quiet any band and silence any talking by a room full of people. His presence was even more magnetic than was that of Hollis'. The thunderous applause and the abrupt attention to anything associated with Charles Boyd was testimony to his ownership of this gathering.

Hollis fidgeted. His facial expression revealed strong discomfort with so much attention directed at him.

Charles moved closer to offer support. "He's already made me extremely proud." He nudged Hollis good-naturedly. "Now he'll have the opportunity to do the same for his country!"

The applause grew more thunderous. Charles, in the manner of a choir director, motioned for quietness. "He just happens to be my favorite son!"

A husky balding lawyer shouted, "And your only son!"

Laughter accompanied the drummer banging the cymbals. "Well, that's beside the point!" Charles responded. There was another clanging of the cymbals accompanied by a drumbeat. He motioned for his son to take the microphone.

"Hollis, are you aware that the whole Tuskegee program will be segregated?" The lawyer persisted.

14

Now the room grew deathly silent. "In other words if there's to be a fighter squadron, it will be composed of Negroes only. Were you aware of that?" Hollis cleared his throat. In a manner that was typical of him he paused as though weighing his answer to make sure that it was right. "No, can't say as I did, Mr. Harper." He was determined to maintain his composure.

"Well, are you going to accept that condition?" Another dancer asked. "I mean, are you still enthusiastic about the whole thing?"

"Affirmative to both questions," Hollis said. He noticed the pride in his father's eyes.

"But you're a real race man," the lawyer continued. "What about those who had their hearts set on flying beside the white boys?"

Hollis paused momentarily. "The way I figure it is that flying with an all-Negro squadron will be much better than not flying at all!"

The applause began as scattered claps and verbal responses.

"And," he continued, "I sure hope enough others think the same way for the project to be a success!"

As the applause grew to thunderous proportions, Charles Boyd pumped his son's hand enthusiastically. The line of well-wishers who followed was continuous.

In Anaheim, California, at nearly the same time, there was another of what would become a nonstop number of Negroes who did not fit according to Buford Saunders. Willie J. Lee was one of these young men. His immediate family was not one of the Negro families that had recently migrated from the South. Rather, his ancestors had come west soon after the Civil War. In fact, one of his uncles on his mother's side had been a member of the famous Ninth Calvary, which, along with the Tenth Calvary, the Indians called Buffalo Soldiers. His father

15

had been one of those Negroes who, with no opportunity to fly with the American Army Air Corps during WWI, had gone to Paris and joined the French Foreign Legion. His attempts to fly with the heroic Lafayette Escadrille, the storied group of men who came from all over the world to be part of this group of romanticists, were financed by some of the wealthiest men in the world. They were not members of the government of America. They were soldiers of fortune volunteering their skills and their intense need to be fighter pilots. Willie J. Lee was a descendent of that stock of men.

Willie climbed out of a roadster containing two ravishingly beautiful women. Coal black and wiry, he approached the military recruiting station excited and bursting with energy that was high, even for one called "Jitterbug" most of his life. So anxious was he to meet with the recruiting non-commissioned officers inside that his feet barely touched the ground.

Inside the recruiting station, a gymnasium-sized room, a line of young white men of all shapes and sizes extended from a long table at the front of the room to the door. Willie had hoped that this time he would see other Negroes beside himself, but no matter. The line was long but he would wait forever if need be. The men looked at him as though he was an aberration. He smiled at the thought.

On his previous visit here he had to wait in line for what seemed like an eternity. He endured expressions ranging from harmless vacuous curiosity to furtive glances to outright resentment. Along with the looks, he endured whispers, chuckles, raucous bawdy laughter, and guarded, forced questions about his presence. There had also been a confrontation with the two sergeants handling the processing. As he moved closer, he saw that the same two were there, and felt like he did when he lined up next to competitors on the starting line at a track meet. His

16

excitement was a boiling cauldron nearly spilling over the edge of its container.

The crusty, chubby one spotted him first and looked him squarely in the eyes. He sipped a cup of coffee, never averting his stare, "Boy," he growled, "what in hell do you want this time?"

Willie nodded, "I'm here to sign up."

The sergeant took a deep breath, looked at the sergeant with fewer stripes sitting beside him as though talking to him rather than to Willie. "For what?"

Willie deliberately opened a copy of the local Negro newspaper to the page displaying a black cadet standing next to an AT-6 trainer airplane. "Same thing the others came to sign up for."

The two sergeants acted as though he had not displayed the newspaper.

The older one said in a measured fashion, "Like I told you before, we ain't looking for midnight fliers. Heard anything to the contrary, Billinsky?"

Billinsky seemed slightly embarrassed. "Can't rightly say that I have."

"I plan to be a fighter pilot," Willie said.

The sergeant stared at him. "Not in my lifetime you won't. Now get the hell out of here before we have to throw you out!"

Willie backed away from the table and with all the drama he could muster, pulled the envelope from his congressman out of his coat pocket, and waved it in the faces of the sergeants. Their expressions were a combination of puzzlement and contempt.

"This is a letter from my congressman informing me that I'm in the Army Air Corps." He could not contain his laughter as he backed away.

The white applicants, now a rapt audience to his performance, gave him room to make his grand exit.

The chubby sergeant was nearly foaming at the mouth as he glared at Willie. His complexion changed from pasty white to a deep red, nearly purple. His attempts at words came out instead as a stutter and sputter like a Model T Ford on a cold morning.

Willie waved the letter dramatically while backing toward the door, thoroughly enjoying the sergeant's display of utter frustration. "Told you I'd be back!" he shouted as he departed.

Outside he climbed into the slick roadster, kissed each of the women, and drove off.

In Columbus, Jordan Wingate rushed home from work anticipating what he might find in today's mail delivery. He walked directly into the front room where his mother always placed the mail. He saw that there was not much to look through today. Junk mail, a bill from the flight school, a letter from a college mate. Perhaps she had not checked the mailbox thoroughly. That sometimes happened. She was getting older, but the mailbox was empty. Twenty-four more hours of frustration. Twenty-four more hours of expecting that the letter would arrive followed by the mental letdown when it didn't. How long could he survive going from one extreme of this emotional pendulum to another? He had been informed that he met all the basic requirements to be accepted. Now if only the letter would come. He swallowed the lump in his throat, fought back the tears starting to form, and jammed a stick of gum in his mouth.

"What you looking for still ain't come?" his father said as he entered the dining room. "Maybe it's 'bout time for you to stop expecting anything from Uncle Sam."

"Never." Jordan tossed the junk mail and bills on the table at which Mose and Annie were playing checkers.

Annie grinned, gap toothed. "Mr. Wingate, I guess your honorable congressman lost your address. And so did the Department of War."

"There's always tomorrow." Jordan headed for the kitchen drawn by the scent of smothered chicken and gravy.

"And there's always today!" His mother met him at the kitchen door. She reached into her apron pocket and handed him the letter he'd been expecting.

His excitement was such that he nearly tore the letter along with the envelope, the first correspondence he had ever received from Washington, D.C. The family gathered around him, eagerly waiting to hear what he read. Jordan looked at them, grinned, and took his time reading it to himself.

"Boy!" his father shouted as he reached for the letter.

"You mean all of y'all want to hear what it says?"

"I think you're about to get hurt, big brother," Annie said.

Jordan laughed. "All right, folks," he said dryly. "It says I've been accepted into the United States Army Air Corps!"

Mose and Annie read it for their satisfaction. Then they yelled, screamed, and hugged Jordan in celebration.

"Boy," Mose said, faking a southern accent, "if the good Lord wanted you to fly, don't you think He'd given you a pair of wings?"

Jordan said, "Guess He's just about ready to do just that. Daddy, you don't know how many times I've heard that one."

"But I sure can guess," Mose said pumping his hand vigorously.

"Hey Jordan," Annie said, "don't you be coming back here a week later complaining about how bored you are."

19

The celebration ceased as they all looked to Jordan as though for confirmation that, unlike so many other ventures he had launched into, this one was something he really wanted.

Sarah's eyes glistened with pride. "My boy will do just fine." She produced a handkerchief and dabbed the tears that flowed freely. "Just fine." Jordan looked into his father's pride-filled eyes. "Daddy, I promise you this is more than just a dream." As he embraced the big man, he felt a boldness unlike he had ever felt before. Three family members were depending on him to take advantage of this opportunity. He resolved not to let them down.

In Washington, D.C., Colonel Buford Saunders escorted Captain George "Hard Rock" Adams into his office. As usual, Buford was not in a good mood. He offered Adams a seat, which he accepted, and one of his favorite cigars, which he refused. Buford thought that one day someone was going to try one of his cigars. Just one is all that he asked. Then they would understand why he liked them so much.

Buford marched pompously around the office, managing to spend a disproportionate amount of time near the painting of himself, always sure to stay within Adams' view. "Well, Captain." He now stood very close, legs spread and arms folded in what he thought was an intimidating pose, looking down at the compactly built man. When Adams finally looked away, Buford was pleased. He sat down. "What did we come up with?"

Adams reached with thick stubby fingers into his briefcase, pulled out a spiral notebook and opened it to a page filled with names and addresses. "Colonel, I'm sure you know that two classes have already started at Tuskegee. One finished."

Buford nodded. "Very small classes."

"But it's a start," Adams smiled.

Buford was not impressed.

"A handful might finish."

"Might." Buford puffed several times on the cigar. "That's a big word, Captain. You got enough names there for a second class?"

"There's quite a few across the country." Adams leafed through the notebook, revealing several more pages of names and addresses. "More Negroes interested than you—than we thought. One from Atlanta named Hollis Boyd. A lawyer. Pretty good grade average in college. He was some kind of boxing champion there."

Buford tossed this information off. "He ever been in an airplane?"

"Let's put it like this. America's in a helluva fix if she's depending on him to protect her."

Buford appreciated Adams' uncharacteristic attempt at humor. "Or if she depends on any of them! Hell we'd be better off training a bunch of chimps. And we wouldn't even have to pay them!" Buford laughed until his face flushed and he broke into a deep smokers' cough that had him wheezing.

"You need anything?" Adams offered, rising from his seat. "Water?"

"Never mind." Buford motioned for him to sit down. "You know I can take care of myself. Since when did I start needing your help, Captain?"

Adams obeyed with obvious reluctance.

Buford did not like what he thought was a smirk on the captain's face. *Cocky bastard,* he thought. "So did you find one out of the whole bunch that had ever been in a plane, not to mention, fly one?"

"A couple of them managed to get into that civilian pilot training program in college."

"I see. A couple, huh? Flying one of those planes is a hell of a lot easier than flying a fighter plane in combat, wouldn't you say?"

"Like comparing riding a thoroughbred to riding a plow horse." Adams' expression indicated he was not sure whether the comparison was appropriate.

Buford shrugged his shoulders. "Well, if so few of them have flown trainers in that program, and the others don't have the slightest idea what the inside of a plane looks like...." Smiling, he puffed on the cigar and blew smoke into the already smoke-filled air.

"There's one in Columbus, Ohio," Adams said.

Saunders waited for him to continue. He grew impatient with Adams' obvious attempt to hold him in suspense. "I understand he's a cut above the rest."

"All right, how much, Captain?"

"A skyscraper compared to bungalows." Adams sipped his coffee. "The reports are that he's a hotshot pilot. Not in the college program. Already graduated."

"So how is he flying?" Saunders' irritation with Adams' piecemeal method of providing information was mounting.

"A civilian flying school." Adams finished his coffee, taking his time. "I heard it's owned by a woman."

Saunders' pondered this information as he arose and crossed over to the window. "Well, most of them haven't learned to fly. And we'll have to make sure this one—"

"Wingate," Adams said.

"Uh huh. We might have to make sure he forgets whatever he's learned. That is if the reports are accurate."

"Sir," Adams seemed to be grasping for the most appropriate words. "You seem real anxious to throw a, uh, damper on this program."

Saunders chuckled. "We don't want them to forget where they came from or where they belong."

"Yes, sir. Sir, I've accepted the assignment at Tuskegee. But did I hear you say 'we' more than once?"

"You heard right, Captain!" Saunders' jaws puffed out. He fixed his eyes on Adams, daring him to show the slightest bit of amusement. "You wouldn't be enjoying yourself would you, Captain?"

"No, sir," Adams responded.

But it was obvious to Saunders that the captain was having to strain to remain serious.

"Absolutely not."

"Good. Remember I'm responsible for your last promotion just as I can be responsible for your next demotion. Now you help me prove those smartass politicians wrong and I'll see that your next move is up the ladder. Deal?"

"Hard to refuse a proposition like that, sir."

CHAPTER THREE

Jordan thought that if first impressions of an area meant anything, the future might be full of problems. As he rode in the bed of the creaky army truck, he reflected on what had happened since he left the Columbus train depot. His first train ride had been an eye opener to say the least. When he boarded the train, he had been allowed to sit in the section that included white passengers. The car he rode was not crowded, thus enabling him to have a compartment to himself. Whites walked past him on their way to other compartments. Because there were so many empty seats, their passing him in favor of another seat did not bother him. The change had come when he reached the Mason-Dixon line and changed trains. At that time he was directed to the last passenger car.

The few Negro men and women on board greeted him. Their curious expressions did not bother him. In fact, they heightened his interest. Their resemblance to many of the Negroes he knew in Columbus reminded him of his mother and father who migrated from Mississippi in the twenties and thirties. They had shared stories with him about the horrors associated with living in the South. Though he had never visited the South before now, whenever he learned that a relative had migrated from there, he asked questions and showed much interest in their stories about what life was like picking cotton and other crops. He had learned years ago that he knew next to nothing about rural living, especially southern rural living. He noticed the plainness and lack of color and frills in the clothing they wore. "Country boy or gal straight out of the cotton fields of 'Sippi'" was the way that he and his friends categorized them. Consequently, during the ride he felt an excitement about the possibilities of meeting Negroes who still lived in the rural environment that spawned his mother, father, and other

24

relatives and friends. He even looked forward to the dirt roads. Many skeptics with whom he talked said locating this particular military program in the South was a guarantee it would fail. They said Negroes from other parts of the country would never adjust to southerners, and neither would white southerners accept Negro officers. This thinking only made Jordan more determined to reach Tuskegee.

The rain began to fall before he arrived at the tiny depot in a town called Chehaw. He understood it was a town, but the depot was all he saw. And the rain fell so furiously, so continuously, he couldn't remember too much of what the depot looked like. All that he knew was that by the time the transportation arrived he was soaked.

He and Claude McCall, a short, tan Negro, rode in silence over the bumpy road leading to Tuskegee. The fall night air and constant drizzle chilled him to the bone. He willed himself to concentrate on keeping his body from shivering and his teeth from chattering.

The truck squeaked, creaked, and bounced over the road, causing the two passengers to hold on to their seats lest they be thrown to the floor, or worse, out of the open end onto the road. The driver seemed set on finding every hill and valley in the road.

"I don't know about you, Mr. Wingate," McCall said, "but if we ever arrive at our destination, I'd just as soon never ride in a military truck again."

Jordan laughed at this cultured fellow from the East Coast whose witty remarks helped him to survive what could have been an unbearable wait in the pouring rain in near total darkness. "At least not on this road," Jordan said.

"That's right. So when we arrive, we immediately request that we get to travel on better roads in better vehicles, and since we're going to make those requests, let's add in better weather."

"We don't want to get too demanding," Jordan said.

"Why not? We'd better get all we can out of white folks while they're in a generous mood."

They arrived at Tuskegee in pitch-black darkness. Here and there yellow lights highlighted a small part of a rough-hewn wooden building. All but one of the buildings that Jordan could see fit that category. The one they stopped in front of was painted white and lit up more than the others. A sign illuminated by lights identified it as the administration building. The driver braked the squeaky truck, which slid in a mud puddle. They felt him climb out of the cab and heard him plod heavily to the back.

"All right, gents," he said in a raspy voice. "Temporary quarters."

They followed him to an unfinished barracks next to the administration building. Inside, cots and lockers were lined up from one end to the other. Just a small percentage of these cots contained mattresses. He handed both of them sheets and enough blankets to shield them from the cool night air.

"Shower in the back. By the way," he said before he left, "tomorrow comes early. Better sleep real fast."

Jordan was not sure about Claude's plans, but he was too tired and cold to do anything but undress and crawl under the blankets.

Morning did come early. Jordan felt someone nudging him. When he opened his eyes, he was staring into the driver's broad grinning face.

"All right, dreamer, it's that time."

Jordan's attempt to pull the blankets over his face was not much of a deterrent to the driver.

"Hey, it's close to seven o'clock. This is like being on a vacation. I heard that when training starts we'll be lucky to see

26

daylight until we've been out of bed a couple of hours."

Claude muttered, "Well, let us enjoy our vacation for the rest of the day, mister."

"Tate. Oscar Tate. Uh huh. If I let you sleep, I've failed the first order I've received as a military man. Is that any way for a future ace fighter pilot to start his career?" Laughing, he jerked the blankets off Claude.

Jordan was up before Tate could do the same to him.

Later, Tate led them through the quagmire that was to become Tuskegee Airfield, their home for the duration of training. The rain stopped falling, but the clouds hung overhead. Tate, in boots and fatigues, seemed well adjusted to the mud. "Your permanent quarters," he said when they arrived at a barracks with an exterior that was still under construction. The interior was much closer to being ready. Ten cots, each sandwiched between a footlocker and wall locker were spaced evenly throughout the barracks with room for more.

"Better get a whole lot of rest before Monday morning, gents," Tate advised them. "That's when all hell will probably break loose!"

Jordan wasn't sure about Oscar Tate. He seemed to get great enjoyment over trying to shock them. The man even laughed maniacally after commenting about how tough the upcoming training would be. Jordan did not expect it to be a bed of roses. If it were, he would be highly disappointed. His parents, especially his father, had preached throughout his lifetime that anything worthwhile would not come easily.

The reverse of that philosophy was that anything that came easily would not have lasting value. In his short life he tried not to do anything that offered a challenge that seemed insurmountable. Or was it that whatever he tried to do he accomplished so quickly, that like his parents said, it bored him so that he was ready to try something else. So the idea that

27

he would be faced with numerous obstacles, some of which might seem insurmountable, was the major reason he wanted to become an ace fighter pilot. If it were difficult then, it obviously would be worthwhile. But Oscar Tate's predictions about the severity of the obstacles to come struck Jordan as being on the fanatical side.

They were kept busy enough during the next four hours to make the time go by quickly and to give them a hint of what the daily life of a cadet would be like. During breakfast they came in contact with members of the class just ahead of them and later, as they attended some orientation classes, they saw cadets jogging through the mud to various training classes.

"Looks like fun," Claude McCall said.

McCall was a different story. In many ways he was unlike any Negro Jordan had ever met. He made comments in an unemotional way and a straight face that had Jordan and others believing him. But seconds later the hint of a grin with a twinkle in his eyes belied what he had said.

Later, Oscar Tate drove them to the Chicken Coop. Neither the inner nor outer appearance of this restaurant/bar/ night club was anything to write home about. Dark, smoke filled, reeking of food, alcohol, tobacco and perfume, it continuously burst at the seams with the many people dancing, eating, drinking, and fighting. But it was much better than anything else in or near the small town of Tuskegee.

Oscar Tate had been there before, without a doubt. Jordan thought that he was a born tourist guide. His enthusiasm there was at the same level as it had been at the airfield. Inside the club the lights were low but the noise was at a high pitch. Several couples were jitterbugging to an upbeat tune played by a lively six-piece band. Some of the observers were clapping and urging the dancers to perform moves more daring than those they were already performing.

"The joint is jumping, hip cats!" Claude shouted so uncharacteristically that Jordan and the others had to make sure the words came from his mouth.

They followed Oscar, who followed a waitress, whose ample buttocks shifted restlessly under her uniform. Oscar was so preoccupied with her buttocks that when she stopped at an empty table he nearly ran into her. "Gentlemen," he said, "this is the best we can offer you."

"Seems like by all the greetings you've been getting you're not a stranger here." Jordan refused the cigarette Oscar offered him.

Claude produced and lit a pipe with a rather large, ornate bowl, filled it with tobacco.

Jordan waved his hands back and forth as if brushing the smoke out of the area.

"I've been here 'bout a month." Oscar puffed on a Camel cigarette while helping Jordan fan away the smoke from Claude's pipe. "Seems like a lot longer than that, though."

"Why so long?" Jordan said.

"Waiting for these folks to find my orders. Or to create some. Whatever they have to do. And before that, I'd waited back home. Little place right outside San Diego, six months for a greeting from my buddy Uncle Sam."

Claude observed Oscar through a jet of smoke. "Would your home happen to be a farm?"

Oscar patted his stomach, flexed the muscles in his ham-like forearm and said, "I've eaten a few pork chops in my life. Why?"

Jordan thought this would be a good time to cut in. "I thought waiting three months for a letter was a hell of a long time." He had made eye contact with a cute young lady with cinnamon complexion, ruby red lips, and a shapely figure. "What about you, McCall?"

"Well, not quite as long as you two." He seemed somewhat embarrassed.

"Damn right," Oscar said.

"All right. About three weeks."

Oscar chuckled. "Guess that's the big advantage of having a daddy who's a politician."

Claude's expression was one of surprise.

"Hey, you can do a whole lot of investigating when you've been here a month. Besides, that little secretary at the University is real, real accommodating."

Jordan decided that the cute young lady was waiting for him to ask her to dance. As he headed in her direction, he noticed Oscar hustling toward another table. The band was playing a love song in a slow, pulsating manner, drawing more couples than the dance floor could hold. Up close, Jordan saw that the female was not as cute as she looked from a distance. Nor was she as young. But the fragrance of her perfume was intoxicating, a welcome contrast to the smell of beer and cigarette smoke. Her body was soft in all of the right places, and she offered not the least bit of resistance when he held her so close their bodies felt like they were welded together.

Jordan noticed Oscar Tate bending a tall, slender woman so far backward he appeared to be trying to bite her huge breasts. And she seemed just as determined not to allow him to succeed. Oscar saw Jordan laughing at him and nodded toward their table, where an attractive woman literally pulled Claude to his feet onto the outer edges of the dance floor. Claude was clumsy, but was dancing well enough to keep up with his partner. But soon the band exploded into a lively number, causing him to flee to the table and leaving her to dance alone.

Jordan was so tickled he had to make a special effort to continue dancing. He noticed that Oscar was having the same problem. In fact, Oscar escorted his partner back to her table until he could stop laughing.

Jordan realized that his partner wanted to continue dancing. He led her into a series of graceful moves, his version of a jitterbug without working up a sweat. No flips or leaps that ended in a split. The audience that gathered around them assured them they were doing fine.

Suddenly Willie "Jitterbug" Lee burst through the front door in a flourish. He was a model of sartorial splendor, wearing a fashionable yellow sports coat over a red shirt open at the neck to reveal a yellow ascot. His baggy green pants complemented the rest of the outfit. So did the yellow spats and gloves. A young woman hung onto each of his arms. One was tall, slender, and wore a haughty expression on her face. The one on the other arm was short, pretty, and vivacious, flashing a smile from the time they entered until they reached the edge of the dance floor. By now they had captured the attention of just about everyone in the room, including the audience that had momentarily belonged to Jordan and his partner.

The audience was spellbound as Willie performed a kind of strip tease, dramatically discarding each glove, his jacket, the ascot, then bending down slowly to remove a spat from around each ankle.

To the delight of the crowd a woman shouted, "Sugar, I don't know how much more of this I can take!"

Willie and his partner performed as if they had been dancing together all their lives. They started off at high speed, causing the band to increase its tempo. Willie whirled the woman around the dance floor a few times. That was only the beginning. The crowd began clapping, encouraging them to try bolder moves. The dancers responded to the challenge bending their slender bodies elastically through a series of exhausting leaps, flips and splits.

Jordan realized that he had been a spectator for some

time now, a role much different from the way he and his partner started off. He escorted her to her table. The music ended and the crowd applauded for what seemed like an hour. Then they were shouting for more. Jordan approached the woman who still held the male dancer's apparel.

"We have an extra seat at our table," he said. He put a bit more emphasis in his smile than might have been necessary.

The woman's smile was two hundred watts, exposing the most pronounced pair of dimples that he had ever seen. As the band blasted off into another high-energy tune, Jordan led her to the table where they joined Claude and Oscar.

Most of the people who had been entertained by Willie and his partner either returned to their tables or, like dance school students, were now eager to put into practice what they had been taught.

Jordan, having learned the name of the man's second escort, and that both she and his dance partner were nurses, wanted to know more about her. The volume the band reached upon the dancer's arrival, along with the near continuous shouting and screams of delight projected by the dancers, made hearing nearly impossible. He leaned close to her. "We might have to carry your friend off the floor if she tries to keep up with him."

Terri Miles flashed the dimples. "Don't you worry about Sue. I guarantee she can more than hold her own on any dance floor."

Oscar chuckled, exposed a mouth full of teeth, which were pronounced against the darkness of his moon-shaped face. "Can't say the same for Mr. Wingate here. Jordan D. Wingate. By the way the 'D' stands for 'David,'" he said with emphasis. Or is it 'Davy'?"

Jordan joined the others laughing. "And Mr. Oscar Tate's middle initial is 'F' as in making *fun* of folks."

Oscar bowed in acceptance.

"My daddy always had this love for anything British-sounding," Jordan continued. "Took on the middle name of Locinvar for himself, and never missed an opportunity to assume the British accent. Especially when he was into the booze."

"Well," Oscar said, "as long as you didn't come down here forgetting who you are, we just might let you stay." He was staring at Claude while he talked. "Ain't that right, Book Man?"

The music ended and Terri motioned to Sue and the dancer to come to their table. The dancer, sweating profusely, bounced toward them. Physically, he and Sue seemed to have been cut out of the same mold. Not an ounce of excess fat on either of their bodies.

"Willie J. Lee," Oscar said. "The man with style, lightning feet, and more women than he knows what to do with! By the way, the 'J' is for 'Jitterbug.'"

Willie beamed. "Sure didn't know my reputation stretched from California to Tuskegee, Alabama!"

Jordan said, "That's because you hadn't met Oscar Tate. He'd make one hell of a private detective."

Indeed, Oscar gave the impression that he knew everything about everybody. Of the cadets Jordan met before Willie, he thought Oscar would certainly make training easier to get through. He somehow obtained background information on each of the fifteen men in their class. He was aggressive and very personable, which no doubt made getting the information an easy task.

After Willie and Sue left the dance floor, the band played slow love tunes. It was as if their energy was connected, as if the two sitting down pulled the plug out of the socket. The reduction of sound made talking easier. Jordan devoted the rest

33

of the evening learning about his future classmates, as well as Sue Banks and Terri Miles, the dimpled one from Beaumont, Texas. As the evening wore on, tongues loosened and barriers of strangers in a strange land for a historical undertaking disappeared.

"What about you, McCall?" Jordan said. "You've said less than anybody at the table."

"I suppose I'm more of a listener. An observer if you will. That is until I get to know people. When I listen to each one of you I realize how boring my life has been."

"Man, you're twenty-four years old," Oscar said.

"That's about right."

"I'm sure that in twenty-four years you've done something we'd be interested in," Sue said.

Claude just shrugged.

But Oscar Tate was not to be denied. "Brother McCall here owns more books than any three libraries."

In spite of the outrageousness of Oscar's announcement, all eyes focused on McCall for his response. His expression was one of embarrassment and of annoyance toward Oscar for insinuating that his love of books diminished his manliness.

Sue eyed Claude in mock seriousness. "Have you read all the books?"

"I bet he sure 'nuff has. Positively," Oscar responded.

Claude's stare changed to a glare at Oscar.

"Then I guess you're what they call a bookworm," Sue continued in a matter-of-fact tone.

"Hey," Willie said, "didn't your professors tell you that too much reading could make you go blind?"

Claude responded to Willie, but his eyes were fixed on Oscar. "No, but they did tell me books could make you smart."

Oscar laughed. "It's good to know that you can talk as well as read, Book Man! Oh, I almost forgot. His father is some kind of politician in New Jersey."

All eyes were on Claude again. He was obviously very uncomfortable. "Friend, we've never lived in New Jersey." He smiled slightly at Oscar. "Better practice on your research."

Everyone laughed. They continued to talk. And by the time they headed back to their barracks, Willie had revealed and bragged about all the records he set on the one-hundred-yard dash in college. Oscar tried to convince the others that getting an education in a small Negro college in the South was a definite advantage. And Claude admitted that having a father who was a politician in Harlem gave him certain advantages in his quest to become a part of this historic program. Unlike the others, he revealed his background with the greatest reluctance.

As they were leaving, Oscar said, "Men of color, I hate to be a messenger of doom, but I've been here long enough to know that the training we're 'bout to get won't be a picnic."

He wasn't wrong. On Monday morning, all hell broke loose.

CHAPTER FOUR

On Monday, the shrill blasts of the whistle came before daylight. Jordan, having spent much time anticipating what a day in ground training would be like, had been unable to fall asleep right away. Willie, Oscar, and he had even played poker well into the morning. The whistle blast came just as he had fallen asleep.

"All right, you girls, beauty rest is over!" A baritone voice boomed. "Time to wee-wee, shower, and climb into those fatigues!"

Throughout the barracks, cadets groaned and cursed as Captain "Hard Rock" Adams stormed from one end to the other. He was shouting, poking cadets, banging on beds and lockers with a stick, and blowing a whistle forceful enough to shatter eardrums.

The sound of Hard Rock's voice and the amount of racket he made prepared Jordan to see a giant of a man. But when he opened his eyes he was startled by the sight of a short, stocky man who could not have weighed as much as he did. He recalled the speckled bantam rooster strutting fearlessly among the pen full of hens in his neighbor's backyard. He also remembered the squat muscular teenager who terrorized the teenagers in Flytown until he, fed up with living in fear, had challenged him. The image of the bullies and the reference to them as females caused him to spring from his bed, landing in a defensive stance that Hard Rock did not notice, or to which he chose not to respond.

They ate breakfast before daylight. At least, those who could eat that early did. Before Jordan had time to digest what was supposed to be eggs, half-cooked bacon, and burnt toast, Hollis Boyd was leading them on a combined run and march under a drizzle of rain. The march began simultaneously with

36

the first sign of daylight.

The rain stopped falling soon after the march began, but the humidity was so high that everyone was sweating profusely. Even the sandy content of the soil could not absorb all the water that was hampering their progress. Occasionally a slight breeze soothed Jordan from the draining heat. He was glad he had kept up a light exercise regimen of walking and running after his football days. An occasional stint of twenty to twenty-five push-ups was the extent of his exercises for the upper body.

"All right, let's take a short rest break, men!" Hollis called out. He spoke his words in a clipped fashion. The grassy areas beside the road were too wet for them to rest there.

Claude said, "I'm going to sit down whether it be in the grass or right here in the mud."

They spread out the rubber-like ponchos, which were fastened onto their belts along with their canteens. These two pieces of equipment were all that they had to carry.

"Don't drink too much water!" Hollis was still standing, still wearing his poncho. "We still have some miles to cover before we're through!" He took a sip of water, then another, as if showing them how to do it.

Jordan took a sip and rinsed out his mouth. Then he swallowed more than a sip. Water never tasted so good.

Willie, squatting on his haunches, tried to spring back up, but his legs were too tired. He sprawled out onto his butt. "Boxer, huh?"

"That's right," Oscar responded. He was sweating more profusely than any of the others. "I heard he was welterweight champ in college."

"Boxing and law sure is a strange combination," Willie continued.

Oscar lit a cigarette. "All I know is he's in damn good shape."

Claude bent over, gasping for air, then staggered around in a circle and finally collapsed onto his poncho. With eyes closed and sweat rolling down his face, he presented a rather frightening picture. Momentarily all eyes were on him. Finally, he struggled to sit up and took much more than a sip of water.

"Hey, watch yourself!" Hollis said. "You want to be sick?"

Claude waited until Hollis strolled out of hearing range. "Gentlemen, you are looking at someone who is not in love with physical training."

"Well, you sure had us fooled," Jordan said.

Humorous comments by the others seemed to enliven Claude.

Hollis, looking as fresh as when the trip began, called "All right, let's move out! We've got a long way to go before we're ready for flight training!"

Jordan was not sure why Hollis had been put in the position of leading the physical training phase of ground training. In conversations during the ten minute rest breaks, he and the other cadets speculated on what, who, or how Hollis acquired his position. According to Oscar Tate, his background was not any more militarily oriented than were any of theirs. He had been in ROTC at Morehouse College in Atlanta. Except for Jordan, most of the others had done the same at the colleges they attended. He had been a champion boxer, which meant that he was physically fit. But so what? Jordan had played basketball and football. Willie had been a better-than-average sprinter. Perhaps it was his southern background. Perhaps not. When they could finally see the base, after five grueling hours of running and marching, they noticed that Hollis Boyd looked fit enough to continue for another six hours. They had to agree that he was the right one.

Hollis Boyd was a different cut than the other cadets.

The difference was obvious from the time he entered the barracks. He declined their offer to accompany them to town, refused to contribute or laugh at their jokes, and said "No" to their invitations to participate in their card games. Even Claude McCall joined in a hand or two of cards before he returned to his books. But not Hollis Boyd.

Colonial Buford Saunders was angrier when he arrived at Tuskegee Army Air Field than he had been just after having received the orders, probably because he arrived totally unprepared for what he saw. He could not remember another instance when he had accepted an assignment that he absolutely hated before he arrived. To make matters worse, this assignment brought him to a hellhole. There was no better way to describe this base in Tuskegee, Alabama. The only other one that could compare with this one was one he served in Europe not too many years after World War I. That base, like this one, had been newly constructed. Then, as now, he had been its first commander, but at least he had commanded white soldiers in that assignment. Having served nineteen years in Uncle Sam's army, Buford refused to look forward to retirement. This assignment could cause him to change his mind.

In his office, he was preparing one of his favorite cigars. He was conscious of Hard Rock Adams watching his every move as though all this was new for him.

"Yes sir, the more I see of this base-in-the-making, the more sure I am that this one is doomed before enough personnel are assigned to wash the dishes," Adams said.

"Don't you worry about that, Captain. We'll be out of this hellhole quicker than you can snap your fingers."

"You really think so?" Adams lit a cigarette.

"Bank on it." Saunders accepted the match and lit his cigar.

Captain Lloyd Kanapka entered and saluted.

39

"Have a seat, Captain," Saunders returned the salute. "Coffee?"

"No, thanks, sir."

Saunders knew that Kanapka, though fairly young, was what military men in-the-know always referred to as a real comer. He knew of his background, which included commanding some difficult units in many of the least favorable locales throughout the United States. He knew that Kanapka's grandfather, Colonel James K. Kanapka, had earned a reputation as a tough, brilliant cavalryman under Theodore Roosevelt in the Battle of San Juan Hill. Though he never met Major Clinton Kanapka, he knew that he was the father of this fair-complexioned, calm-looking captain sitting across from him. He couldn't help comparing his appearance with the gruff, hard look of Adams sitting next to him. They were the exact opposite in appearance, background, and he was sure in other ways. Saunders was interested in their toughness, in their ability to take orders from him. In that way they were alike.

"Since you men have already met, let's get on with the business at hand." He strolled back and forth. Glancing out his window, he saw a group of cadets marching into view. Even from this distance they didn't appear sharp.

"Men, we're here to perform a miracle too hard for the great God Almighty himself to perform." He chuckled, as he usually did, whenever he said something he thought was humorous. He noticed a trace of a smile on Adams' face. Not so Kanapka. His expression was as inscrutable as it always was. Not having elicited the response he desired, he decided against sitting down. Make them pay attention by moving. "What do you think of your new assignment, Captain Kanapka?"

"Well, sir, I—"

"Don't worry." Buford sat down. "I know how you feel." He laughed and broke into his deep nicotine induced

40

cough. "Wondering what damn crime you committed to deserve this kind of punishment."

Adams laughed, looking to Buford for approval, but Buford knew that the laugh was hollow.

Kanapka was definitely uncomfortable. "Sir, as a matter of fact, I–"

"You climbed up the ranks fast. Damned fast. Had some tough assignments."

"Yes, sir."

"But, son," Buford said as he rose, "you ain't seen nothin' yet!" He was on stage again. "Sometimes in your career you have to take an assignment that you feel is a total waste. About like being told your job is to move manure from one spot to another eight hours a day! With a shovel the size of a tablespoon! I mean, 'Nigras' flying!" He saw that the cadets were in formation just outside one of the barracks.

Jordan's attention to daily exercise stood him in good stead during most of the morning march and run, but not totally. They covered ten miles, and even the frequent ten-minute breaks did not prevent the ache in his legs nor the blister on his left foot. The ache had begun when they reached the three quarter mark, but he was determined not to complain. Claude McCall complained enough for all of them. Often during the torturous journey, they came to Claude's aid, steadying and supporting him. Two of them carried him on their backs a time or two. Another cadet named Larry Jackson needed the same kind of support. With one mile to go, the cadets' complaints increased. They followed their complaints with proposed remedies for their various sources of discomfort, remedies such as sleep, rest, lavish meals, and long vacations. Jordan could feel soothing hot water from the shower caressing every muscle in his body.

"All right, cadets," Hollis shouted. "Fall out!"

"Wait just a minute! Cadet Boyd," a voice bellowed, "what in hell are these boys, these girls, training for?"

Jordan turned and saw a group of white officers moving quickly, nearly running toward them as if they had committed a crime.

"To be fighter pilots, sir!" Hollis responded.

Then all hell broke loose. The six officers were led by the short, compact one whose voice reminded Jordan of someone speaking through a handheld megaphone at a sporting event.

"Push-ups!" he shouted. "How many can they do? Never mind! Assume the position, girls, and give me ten, no, twenty push-ups!"

As Jordan and the others forced their weary bodies into the prone position, the officers, led by the short officer, swarmed into their ranks. Most of them were civil, but the short one filled the air with taunting and cursing.

"Fighter pilots!" he shouted. "Dumb-ass thumb-suckers is what they are! You call those push-ups! Raise your big guts off the ground. We need to send all of you back to Africa!"

After strutting back and forth through the ranks, he silently inched close to Claude McCall. "Who in hell do we have here?" He stood with his hands on his hips like a rooster primed to enter into battle. "Or should I ask what do we have?"

"McCall, sir," he said. His effort to keep from falling flat on his stomach sapped his strength so that his voice was nearly inaudible.

"Who? Sound off like you've got a pair of balls!" Hard Rock's voice blasted through the air overwhelming any other sound. He looked toward the older officer standing on the side,

42

arms folded like a coach watching his players.

"Smart boy." The short one kicked Claude's shaky arms out from under him, leaving him face down in the mud. Then he leaned down close and shouted, "Call your pappy to help you! That is, if you've got one!"

Claude's expression was a mixture of humiliation, anger, and fear. He righted himself and tried to do a push-up. It was obvious to everyone that he would not succeed.

"All right, Cadet Boyd. What else can they do?"

Hollis shouted, "Cadets, on your feet. Run in place!"

Jordan had overcome the aches in his legs and feet and had performed the push-ups and pull-ups seemingly with no effort. Now he could feel the eyes of the runt of an officer penetrating his skin.

"And who do we have here? Or better still, what do we have here?"

Jordan, having gotten a second or perhaps a third wind, kept running, lifting his knees higher than before. "Wingate!" he responded, having no way of anticipating what was to follow. Suddenly, he was being confronted, surrounded by the short officer and three of the others.

"Wind Gate?" Hard Rock shouted. The others echoed his name.

"Where in hell did you get a name like Wind Gate?" He laughed derisively. And the others echoed the laughter.

"Wingate, Jordan!" Jordan said. His legs were nearly numb, but he was determined to maintain his composure.

Hard Rock was so close he was nearly touching Jordan. "Wind Gate Jordan? Which name comes first, boy? Don't matter. We'll see how much wind you've got! Drop and give me twenty push-ups!"

Jordan hesitated momentarily, dropped into a perfect push-up posture, knocked off ten easily, but struggled,

43

breathing laboriously through the second ten. He burned inside as he performed on pure instinct, pride, and, most of all, stubbornness, alternately running in place and doing push-ups in response to Hard Rock's goading and the other officers' laughter. From somewhere, seemingly far away, he could hear Hard Rock's shouting, his voice sonorous for someone of such small stature.

"You stupid bastard! Forget about being a fighter, pilot until you learn to respect your superiors! The answer is "Wind Gate, sir! Sir! Sir! And don't you forget it!"

Jordan was too exhausted to respond verbally even if he wanted to.

"Get him the hell out of here!" Hard Rock said. Then Jordan felt the arms of others supporting him.

"Cadet Boyd," Hard Rock continued. "What you have here is one tit-sucker, a bunch of cotton-pickers, and one pig-headed clown! You're charged with whipping them into perfect physical condition! If not, I'll ship all of you out of here before you even see an airplane! I make myself clear?"

"Yes, sir!" Hollis responded.

In the barracks, after everyone had showered, Jordan later than the others, they were getting dressed and discussing the confrontation with the white officers. There was still more daylight left than had passed.

"What in hell did you do to that son of a scorpion?" Claude asked Jordan.

"Adams," Oscar informed the group. "Captain 'Hard Rock' Adams. I don't think I remember his first name."

The others looked at him in mock disbelief.

Oscar smiled, "Oh, I just remembered. It's George. He was a hell of a fighter pilot in World War I. Damn, Jordan. He and the rest of those white boys attacked you like German Shepherds on an alley cat."

44

Jordan struggled to his feet and forced himself to move around, lest his muscles get so sore that he could not move. "I've always heard that cats have nine lives."

Willie Lee put the finishing touches on his boots. The toes and heels were gleaming. "Tell you what, Hotshot," he said to Jordan, **"I was sure you'd just about reduced yours to eight."**

Jordan tossed that off. He was moving better in spite of the soreness. "What you Negroes need is just a little more faith in yourselves. Columbus guys don't break. We're tough as nails. You've got to realize that these white folks are sure enough going to see what you're made of."

Oscar said, "Yeah, providing we stay alive long enough for them to find out."

The laughter in response to Oscar's remark was the first good laugh they had all day and it did much to relieve the tension.

A gangly, middle-aged Negro civilian carrying a toolbox in one hand and a plunger in the other exited the latrine and ambled toward them.

"Gents," Oscar said, "Meet Slide Rice. Mr. Walter 'Slide' Rice. He's the chief fix-it man on the base. They say that he can fix whatever's broke. Don't matter what it is. The only reason he wouldn't be able to fix it is because it wasn't really broke. Just looked like it was."

Slide smiled exposing two bad teeth in the front.

"Heck of a nickname," Willie said as he shook Slide's hand.

As Jordan shook hands with Slide, he remembered that a favored uncle's hands had the same rough, leathery feel. Years ago, before suffering a permanent crippling injury, he had displayed the same skills.

"You boys some more of them pilot trainees?" Slide's

45

voice was soft. He had apparently smiled so much his dark face contained permanent laugh lines. "The other trainees seem to be getting along right nicely. But . . . ." A slight frown replaced the smile. He seemed to be searching for the appropriate word.

"That so, Mr. Rice?" Willie said. "They haven't run into trouble with the white folks down here? The officers?"

Slide pondered this awhile. Then the smile returned. "I wouldn't go that far now. They probably don't like you boys, mostly from the North. If you boys want to get along down here you sure 'nuff got to understand the ways of the white folks."

The other cadets in the barracks stopped whatever they were doing and gravitated toward Slide.

Oscar said, "Anybody ought to know how to get along with white folks it's got to be Slide Rice."

Slide decided at that particular moment to stroll softly to the opposite side of the barracks in search of some item. In doing so he left the cadets in a state of surprise, frustration, and humor. There was stone silence until he found the item, a screwdriver. The cadets waited as he took as long to return as he had to retrieve the screwdriver.

"My first day here," Oscar said, "Slide taught me a good lesson."

Jordan and the others moved in closer.

"I couldn't even put my bags down before the white boys were ordering me to clean out all the toilet bowls in sight. I was mad as hell. But you know what?" He paused to add a bit of suspense. "Slide convinced me to do it. Told me not to overlook one bowl."

Oscar's facial expression and tone of voice connoted an excitement that seemed out of place.

"In your civilian clothes?" Jordan said.

Oscar smiled and nodded.

Then all eyes turned to Slide who responded with a

smile. "He's still here, ain't he?"

"You've got a point," Jordan said amidst a few chuckles from the cadets.

"Tell you what else old Slide did for me," Oscar continued in his exaggerated excitement. "The very next day the white folks wanted me to clean every pot and pan in the mess hall until you could see your face in them!"

The cadets, now aware that Oscar was having fun, joined in with laughter and prodding.

Willie said, "And Slide did what?"

"Hell, he convinced me to do it. What else?"

"What else?" came a chorus of responses. All eyes turned to Slide.

Slide smiled and said, "He's still here, ain't he?"

The cadets could hardly contain themselves from rolling on the floor with laughter.

Jordan moved close to Slide, and presenting his most serious facial expression said, "So, Slide, I guess if they'd worked poor Oscar to death and buried him in one of those fields out there you'd still say---"

The other cadets joined Jordan in a loud response, "He's still here, ain't he?"

Hollis Boyd entered the barracks and saw cadets holding their sides and rolling on the bunks and on the floor with laughter. He paused just inside the door.

Slide Rice waited until the laughter and the remarks subsided. "Hold it one minute, young fellas." His mood was serious.

"Okay, Mr. Slide," Willie said, "lay it on us about how to get along with the white folks down South."

Although Hollis was born and raised in the South, he moved closer, listening intently to Slide.

"Just don't be too slow 'bout lettin' him know who's

boss, that's all." Slide picked up his toolbox and a can of paint and shuffled out of the barracks, passing Hollis Boyd on the way out.

"All right, men," Hollis said, "you've got about two minutes before the next formation!"

CHAPTER FIVE

Jordan Wingate was not sure whether he liked the way things were shaping up at Tuskegee Army Airfield. For two weeks, the sky seemed as though it had leaks in it. The rain wreaked havoc with much of the outdoor training, yet Captain Kanapka, Captain Adams, or Hollis Boyd usually decided that they would participate in physical training, rifle target practice, or compass orientation. Most of the base was still under construction. With no roofs to protect workers from the rain, construction came to a standstill. Finally, the good Lord apparently decided that these Negro cadets needed to finish ground training if they were ever going to get familiarized with airplanes. Therefore, He had closed the leaks in the sky. Two weeks of heavy, near nonstop rain were more than enough to convince Him that indeed, the State of Alabama had gotten its share. But the weather was not Jordan's biggest concern. Everyone complained about that. People were his major concern.

Hard Rock Adams was relentless in what Jordan described as a crusade to get rid of him. Before he fully recovered from the first confrontation, he was faced with a second and a third. Just when he thought he would be able to get through his training like the other cadets, he was singled out again. He could be walking across the base minding his own business, feeling confident that he was adjusting to military life when Adams would shout out his name, sometimes from as far as three blocks away. It was said that Adams' lungs must be made of iron or at least leather. As Jordan stood at attention, Adams would parade toward him like George C. Cohen prancing across a Broadway stage. Jordan spent a good deal of time standing at attention waiting for the stocky little captain to approach. "Wind Gate!" Adams called his name that way so

49

often, and from so many areas of the base, that it became a topic of conversation by members of his class, as well as those in the previous class. Adams, in effect, changed Jordan's middle name from David to "Wind." What had him so confused was that Adams was not their official commander during basic training.

Captain Lloyd Kanapka was a different story. Though it was obvious by his accent that he, like the other officers, was a Southerner, he treated the cadets in a much more humane way. Jordan's impression of Kanapka was that he cared. The others felt the same way. Although ground training was a bore, its end would mean the beginning of flight training and a rumored changeover from Kanapka to Hard Rock Adams.

Finally, there was Cadet Hollis Boyd. For some reason, whenever there was a need for one of the cadets to lead their group to and from a class, Hollis got the nod. Whenever the cadets were engaged in training, he was chosen to lead. Whether the matter was a clean-up detail, physical training, or when Kanapka or Adams wanted something done, Cadet Hollis Boyd's name was called. On the other hand, Jordan's name was called when something went wrong.

"The question is this," Oscar sidled up to Jordan in the mess hall. "It's not what you did to Hard Rock, but what in hell have you done to all of the white folks? Maybe we ought to go up top to Bulldog." Bulldog was Oscar's nickname for Colonel Buford Saunders.

"What do you think he'll do? I mean if he hasn't done anything yet and we're finishing ground training I don't know if we can expect anything more."

"How do you know he knows?" Oscar continued. "We don't see him that much."

"We see him enough." Jordan stretched his legs. In the time since they'd arrived, he felt he had done enough walking and running to take off from Tuskegee and walk to Columbus in a moment's notice.

"My thoughts are that if you've got five or six officers under you they have to be carrying out your orders, your philosophy."

Claude sat down beside them. He was quiet, seemingly in deep thought. "Well Wingate," he said, "I'm just glad you've been here all along. Not that I've enjoyed you having to take all of the heat."

Oscar laughed. "But better him than you, right, Book Man? The only reason you're still here is because for some reason, the officers have spent most of their time making life miserable for Hotshot."

Claude bristled. "You know what, if I ever thought of quitting, it wouldn't have as much to do with Wingate as it would with me being determined to stay here longer than you!" He was defiant in the face of Oscar Tate's cynicism. "Tate!" he said as he arose, "I'll be here as long as you. Even longer!"

Oscar did nothing but mock Claude's serious expression and laugh just a little more emphatically than he needed to.

Later, Captain Kanapka approached them as they stood in formation outside their barracks. "Men, you've just completed the easy part of your training!"

Out of the corner of his eye, Jordan noticed Hard Rock and two lieutenants approach the formation.

Captain Kanapka continued, "On Monday morning you start the first phase of flight training!"

Hard Rock and the others stopped some fifteen feet to the side of Kanapka. If Kanapka saw him and the others, he gave no indication.

"Have a good weekend! Fall out!"

The cadets let out a yell of gratification, finally able to relax for a short time. They started toward the barracks.

"Class, attention!" It was the familiar drone of Hard

Rock. "Hear me well, girls. I don't give a damn what you do between now and 0400 hours Monday morning. But come that hour, I want your asses here ready to go! Fall out!"

Jitterbug said, "I'd say we jumped out of the frying pan and into the fire."

Jordan thought that might be putting it mildly. After spending weeks being in near constant odds with Hard Rock, could he put up with him through who knew how many months of flight training? Well, he had made it through one phase, enduring more harassment than during his entire life. During that time, he wrote and sent at least two letters to his family. Like most of the cadets, his contact with them was just as he expected it to be. His daddy wanted to know whether the military people there were the real thing or merely impostors. In essence, was he really serving Uncle Sam? And was he really training to be an Army Air Corps pilot? Had he flown or even seen a plane? His sister wanted to know whether he was still committed or already bored. If not yet, how long would it be before he did get fed up and decide that he needed a new challenge? His mother stood firm in her belief that the good Lord would do great things for and through him.

Just as Jordan and the other cadets discovered the first night at the club, Oscar Tate was the cadet that kept everyone loose during the toughest times. This chunky, thick-necked young man was from a broken family and had grown up in the cotton fields of a small town in Arkansas. He lived his high school and college years in San Diego, California, and was always the pill for whatever ailed their class. No matter how difficult physical training got, Oscar Tate provided humor to make it bearable. No number of push-ups was too many. No amount of setups too strenuous, nor were their runs too long. Oscar brought wit to the most frustrating situation.

Jordan thought about Cadet Claude McCall. If there was one cadet that the others had doubts about, it was Book Man. Tate's whipping boy, the butt of his jokes, had apparently gotten past his constant frustration of needing to tell Tate where to go or where to stick it. If Tate made him mad, he reached the point where he held his anger in check by keeping silent. But the anger showed in his eyes, lips, and clenched fists. Sometime during ground training, he determined that the only way to get along with Cadet Oscar Tate was not to take anything he said personally and to realize that no one was immune to his barbs. When that realization came, the cadets saw a new person. They saw Cadet Claude McCall, rather than simply Claude McCall.

Cadet Willie Lee was much more than the loose-jointed dancer sporting flashy clothes and women clinging to him. He was more than the happy-go-lucky-never-having-lost-a-one-hundred-yard-dash man. He was not on the same level as Oscar Tate when it came to needling, but he wasn't far behind. Willie's value to the group was his constant carefree manner. Unlike Oscar, who at times could be surly, Willie was always cheerful. Also unlike Oscar, whose needling could sometimes have an irritating effect, everyone could count on Willie's good nature. Whereas Oscar often used his humor as a weapon to stir someone up, to get back at them, or as a shield to protect himself, humor was Willie's normal disposition.

Hollis Boyd was the most difficult cadet for Jordan and the others to understand. Not since Jordan left home had he met anyone as religious. It wasn't just that Hollis read the Bible all the time. That was there for all of them to see. What distinguished Hollis was his mannerisms, his way of conducting himself. It was what he did not do more than what he did, what he did not say rather than what he said. He was the calm, clear-thinking lawyer, the Southern gentleman born, raised, and educated in Atlanta, Georgia. He was the no-nonsense cadet who approached every aspect of ground training as if it were the last chance he would have to do so. Whatever he did, it was obvious to Jordan that he wasn't doing so on the spur of the moment.

Although Jordan was rivaling Hollis in every phase of their ground training, Hollis was the one singled out by the white officers for areas of responsibilities. Jordan and the others learned to expect that. They singled him out to be the unofficial leader of their small class of cadets. Some of the cadets were not too appreciative of the selection. Jordan was one of the least appreciative, primarily because of how the other cadets, as well as the officers, seemed to automatically pit him against Hollis.

Jordan was accustomed to competition. It was something he had thrived on since his days as a star running back in high school, but this was different. This was a team in the making. All it needed was for players in different positions to come together for the team to be complete. This was an underdog operation of the biggest proportions and they were trying to prove that if given the opportunity they could become successful fighter pilots. Yet in the midst of this struggle, one of the prospective team members was showing signs of remaining an outsider.

Jordan believed in individuality, so he had to ask himself what was it about Hollis Boyd that bugged him? Was it that Captains Kanapka and Adams placed Hollis in a sort of unofficial leadership position? Was it the clean, holierthanthou attitude and lifestyle? Was it his ritualistic Bible-reading, practiced before the wake up whistle every morning and before he went to bed? At least McCall's reading material had more variety.

He decided that it wasn't the time to worry about

personalities. This would be the first weekend that they were given enough time to travel to Montgomery, Alabama. Jordan and Willie joined Oscar tuning up his Ford for the trip. Besides Hollis, Oscar was the only cadet in the class to have a car. Military rules prevented them from driving during the preliminary phase of training. Despite the age of the Ford, Oscar had kept it in good shape.

Jordan lay awake that night thinking about all that he and the others had endured during ground training. He thought about his mother, father, and sister. Regardless as to how coolly the old man acted when Jordan broke the news about completing ground training, Jordan knew he was smiling. True, Jordan had not even started flight training. Still, he had put himself in a position to begin. One phase at a time was his motto. He heard Oscar and several other cadets snoring. Oscar was always the loudest. He heard Willie rolling from side to side, grunting, moaning, and emitting other strange noises. Jordan never required much sleep. And when he did sleep he would be awakened by the slightest noise. He was familiar with the sleeping patterns of each of his barrack mates, including Hollis. Hollis slept soundly, nearly silently. He lay still, as organized in his sleep as he was during the day. Jordan's last thoughts before falling asleep were of getting away from Hard Rock Adams for two whole days. It was a most pleasant thought by which to fall asleep.

Saturday morning the sun shone brightly and there was no sign of rain. They would have a nice drive. Jordan entered the latrine as Willie was finishing his shave. Oscar and Claude followed Jordan into the latrine. By 8:00 they were rushing out of the barracks. They weren't the first ones to do so. All they had to do was pick up Terri Miles and they would be off to Montgomery. They were ready to go, but unfortunately the car wasn't.

"Could've sworn the Black Chariot had all of its parts last night," Oscar said. He was looking under the hood touching, pulling various parts. "Especially spark plugs and battery cables. No telling what else is missing." Aided by Jordan and Willie, he continued his check.

They didn't find anything else wrong. The remaining parts of the Ford were intact. The question was where to get a couple of spark plugs and battery cables.

"Simple. Not a real problem," Claude informed them. "We borrow them from one of the military vehicles."

They looked at Claude like he was a little crazy and continued to question where they might find the parts. They spent very little time speculating on who the automobile parts culprit could be.

Walter "Slide" Rice came to their rescue. He found the parts right away, but when he stepped on the gas pedal nothing happened. "Boys, I reckon we just might have us a clogged-up gas line."

Oscar and the others left the base at 3:00. They thought about alternative routes to Montgomery, but the others were narrower than the main route. The delay caused them to drive when traffic was heavier than it would have been during the early morning hours. They passed the *Welcome to Montgomery* sign with very few daylight hours left. The signs of racial separation were much more evident in Montgomery. Negroes were assigned their own drinking fountains, their own toilets, their own restaurants, even their own cemeteries and medical centers. Still, just as was true in Tuskegee, the streets of Montgomery were teeming with Negroes.

When they reached the washed-out gray wooden house where they were to meet Sue Banks, a relative informed them that she had suffered a bad accident and was at the doctor's office.

On the way, the relative, a teenager named Lizzie, explained to them the accident occurred on a bus just after noon. Jordan remembered how the problem with the car had delayed their arrival, but it was too late to worry about that. The expressions on the faces of the other cadets, as well as the sound that escaped Terri's mouth, let him know that they were thinking similar thoughts, that the accident was not really an accident.

From the outside, the doctor's office looked a little like a shack. The inside was clean with the antiseptic smell of a hospital. It was packed with Negroes of all ages who were there for treatment of a gamut of illnesses and injuries. One of two nurses led them to what served as the emergency room where Sue lay on a cot. A sheet covered her body. The whole left side of her face resembled that of a mummy.

The nurse, short, attractive, and obviously overworked lingered, making sure that Sue was comfortable. "Darn police anyhow," she said just above a whisper. Then she left the room.

They could not get an accurate account of what had actually happened to Sue. She was in too much pain and too anesthetized to communicate with anyone. The doctor's report said the accident happened as she was exiting the bus. She tripped on another passenger's foot, tumbled head first into the stairwell where she hit the door. Terri insisted that Sue should be released and transported back to the hospital near Tuskegee Airfield. Her condition was such that everyone decided to forego the Sunday of their two-day weekend. Terri rode with her in a car that Sue's cousin drove.

"Do you buy that story?" Jordan said to the other cadets. Willie said, "Not the way that woman can dance. I can hardly believe she'd be clumsy enough to trip over somebody's foot and not catch her balance. The little bit of her face that you could see looked like she'd just boxed ten rounds against Joe Louis."

Jordan said, "I think we should try to find out what really happened."

"Meaning what?" Oscar said.

"That the local police department ought to have the report." He was conscious of Oscar's hesitancy. The other cadets did not seem to be any more willing to agree with him than Oscar was. "Look, it shouldn't be that hard to trace this thing and find the policeman that filed this report . . . then we—"

"Wait a minute, Hotshot," Claude said. "Listen to what the man is saying."

"Yeah, Hotshot. Oscar knows more about the South than all of us together," Willie added.

But Jordan had made up his mind. "All I want to do is make sure that the story about how Sue came to look like she'd been run over by a truck is true. I can't see anything wrong with that. Can any of you fine American military cadets honestly see anything wrong with that?"

"Jordan, answer me one question." For once Oscar was dead serious. "I ask you again. Do you know what part of the country we're in?"

Jordan nodded. "And I know what year this is. Slavery ended with the Civil War, I thought. Time for us to remind these folks of that. And I know who we are, and that we'll be expected to fight for this country, including the dear old South." He was starting to walk away from them, hoping all the time that they would follow. They did.

Later they entered the local police station. There were two officers there. As it was near midnight, the heavyset officer seated at the desk was obviously fighting sleep. As Jordan, followed by the others, entered, the heavyset one sat up straight and instinctively opened the chest drawer. The other policeman, short, pimply, sallow cheeked, followed them, his hand resting on his gun handle.

"What do you boys want?" The heavyset one stood up.

"A woman friend of ours had an accident," Jordan said. "On a city bus."

The big one looked at him like he was crazy. His response was simply a shrug of his beefy shoulders. He gazed quickly at each one of them until his eyes rested on the policeman of lesser rank, obviously a signal for the latter to draw his weapon.

In the midst of stone silence, Jordan shivered in fear of being alone and defenseless before two Southern white policemen armed and obviously not too happy about them being there.

"A woman," he repeated.

"You boys know it's after midnight. You're asking for lots of trouble when you come barging in here at this time. Hell, at any time." The big one's face was beet red.

"We're in the military, sir," Oscar said.

Jordan had never heard him speak so softly or so timidly.

"All right let me see some identification. Place it right on that desk real nice and easy." His voice, posture, and facial expression were a dare, a challenge for them to make a wrong move. He took his time surveying the cards and insisting that the other officer do the same. "You boys know there's military police in this city?" The irritation in his voice increased.

"We do, sir," Oscar said, motioning to the others that this was a cue to leave.

The big officer said, "I got a mind to call them up and charge you with trespassing."

Oscar assured him that taking that measure would not be necessary. He, Willie, and Claude headed for the front door.

Jordan hesitated, noticed that the policemen were growing angrier, and followed the others.

Later, Oscar tailed the green Chevy carrying Sue to the hospital. "Welcome to the South," he said bitterly. "New territory for Sue just like it is for the rest of you gents. I'd like to know more about that policeman that filed that 'accident' report. And I sure would like to know what happened on that bus."

"So you sense foul play?" Claude said.

"That's what I sense, Book Man. Sure do. I hate to say it but what we just witnessed is a bit of Southern justice."

The rest of the trip was made in silence.

They did not have to travel out of their way to get to the hospital where Terri had driven Sue. After they were satisfied that she would recuperate fairly soon, they returned to the base.

When they entered the barracks, Hollis was shining his boots. He approached them, a concerned expression filling his handsome face. He focused on Jordan. "Captain Adams is looking for you cadets."

The person looking for them was actually Colonel Buford Saunders. Adams was there simply as a silent bystander, a spectator who, along with Jordan, Claude, Willie, and Oscar, was there to witness Saunders' pre-speech performance. As the cadets stood at attention, Saunders stood with his back to them, shifting his cigar from one side of his mouth to the other. He puffed a time or two on the cigar. Then he strolled to his desk and doused it without looking at the cadets. He had not done so since they arrived. "Captain Adams," he drawled, "is everybody here that should be here?"

Jordan could swear that out of the corner of his eye he could see a hint of a smile in Hard Rock's eyes.

"Yes sir. All present and accounted for."

"Good." Saunders kept them at attention while he strolled back and forth. "Listen to me closely. You boys are here for one thing, and one thing only. That's to get through this training so as to serve your country. Correct me if I'm wrong." For the first time, he peered into each one of their eyes, lingering at each stop. "Then your asses belong here on this damned base, not in town. Sure in hell not in Montgomery. I make myself clear?" Until now his voice had been in a conversational tone, but now he shouted, "I said, do I make myself clear?"

Jordan and the others were startled into an affirmative response.

"Good!" Saunders shouted. "Now get the hell out of here while you can! Everybody but you, Cadet Wingate!"

Jordan was singled out to dig a ditch six feet wide, six feet long, and six feet deep. This time Saunders assigned the punishment rather than Adams. However, because Adams was assigned to make sure the command was completed, Jordan saw it no differently than any of the other punishments or, as the officers preferred to label them, 'disciplinary actions.'

Just when Jordan was on the verge of accepting more discipline without knowing why it was being administered, Saunders ordered Adams and him to halt.

"You'd best consider yourself damn lucky that you got back to this base in one piece." For an instant, the look in his eyes was one of extreme hatred. "The matter with that woman was a civilian matter. It was to be taken care of by non-military officers of the law. They've been handling matters like that very capably all these years, but you seem to think you can do it better. Smartass 'Nigra' from the North. That's what you are, right?" He moved his face uncomfortably close to Jordan's. He was a blazing hot potbellied stove that needed to cool down. He started to pick up a cigar, then, as if making sure that he continued in the same mood, he put it down.

61

Jordan was relieved that he didn't have to smell the odor of the cigar up close. Being splattered by the spit that escaped the colonel's wide mouth was torture enough.

"When you or any other cadet here has a problem of such major proportions, the Military Police is who you take it to. I don't know that what you stuck your nose in was worth getting city police department in an uproar. But that's what you did, Cadet! That's what the hell you did!"

Jordan wanted to get this over with before he either puked or had to wipe Saunders' saliva off of his face.

"I'm not sure you even belong in this program. Seems to me the only thing you're good for is causing a whole lot of trouble. Believe me if there's one more incident I'll have your ass out of here heading back to wherever you came from. I make myself clear?"

"Yes, sir!"

Getting away from Colonel Buford Saunders' spit and foul breath was more important than worrying about digging a hole in the ground. Eight weeks of ground training should have prepared him to handle that. Disturbed, he followed Hard Rock and a rangy, lantern-jawed lieutenant to the site for the digging, but determined to play their games. Being physically fit was a great strength.

He found that trying to dig a hole with nothing more than the small shovel issued to each cadet was not as easy as he thought it would be. Just after noon on a muggy day, the sun beating down unmercifully, his first jabs of the shovel proved to be no problem. The large amount of rain had softened the soil, but time was his enemy. Nearly an hour after he began digging, the muscles in his arms, shoulders, and back were throbbing.

The lieutenant granted him a ten-minute break. Jordan took some sips of water from his canteen. It was warm but it relieved the dryness. He had been digging so long that he relished the idea of stretching his body and legs. He walked back and forth and in a circle around the hole. Adams arrived just as he was considering sitting down.

"Wind Gate, it shouldn't take you all day to get that hole dug! My five year old could do it in half the time it's taken you to dig that little piss-hole. So I know a lazy-ass like you can do it in at least three hours. Looks to me like you'll have to get busy if you expect to meet my deadline. Let me tell you I'm not too happy with anybody who can't meet my deadlines. You understand, Wind Gate?"

"Yes, sir!" Jordan watched Adams strut away, leaving him at the mercy of the quiet, inscrutable lieutenant, the heat, aching muscles, and what was left of his three-hour deadline.

Late that night, after several hot showers, a meal, and a soothing massage by Claude, Jordan forgot about the soreness long enough to fall asleep.

The next morning Hard Rock Adams was conducting a class on aircraft identification. Previously the classes were held in a room and the airplane was a diagram with each part labeled clearly enough for a cadet in the back row to read it. This class, however, was being held outside, next to an airplane. Adams brandished a shiny metal pointer like it was a magic wand, pointing at different parts of the PT-17 trainer airplane. They had been told that they were to have committed the parts to memory by this day.

Jordan's eyes swept over the other cadets. He already knew which ones were prepared and which ones were not. The extent of concern in their eyes supported that knowledge. So did the degree of squirming by each of them under the scrutiny of Hard Rock's small black eyes peering out from under his thick black eyebrows, and that continuous drone that sent shivers up and down their spines.

"Girls, don't even think of flying one of my planes

until you can identify every part down to the smallest screw!" He focused on each cadet in a dramatic fashion, stopping at Claude, the tip of his wand touched the nose gear on the plane. "And what, pray tell, is this, Cadet?"

"A front wheel, sir!"

"Idiot!" Adams shouted after a lengthy silence. "Have you ever flown anything before?"

"No. No, sir."

Adams looked at two officers standing at the edge of the class. Throwing up his hands and rolling his eyes in a gesture of helplessness, he said, "This is the one that couldn't do one damn push-up without crying for his pappy!" He got nose to nose with Claude. "Can you do anything?"

"No. Yes, sir!" Claude was shaking noticeably.

"The next time you call any part of my airplane a front wheel you can start packing your bags. Is that understood?"

"Yes, sir!"

Adams looked over to the other officers. "And to think this is one of the smartest ones in the bunch." He strutted some more. "Can any one of you college boys help Cadet Smartass?"

None of the other cadets responded. Although Jordan knew the answer, he wanted to remain as inconspicuous as possible. *Let someone else take the heat.* The only sound was Adams tapping his pointer on the plane, the floor, and against his thigh as he walked through the ranks. Even when Jordan could not see him he could feel his eyes.

"Wind Gate thinks he just might know."

"It's the nose gear, sir!" Another pause. Jordan felt good knowing he not only had the right answer, but also that he had shown the right military courtesy. After the ditch digging episode and hearing Saunders suggest that being washed out of the program early was not beyond the realm of possibility, he abandoned some of his loose, devil-may-care attitude. If he was going to wash out, he preferred that it be for poor performance rather than a nebulous charge about a lack of respect.

"Lucked out on the answer, didn't you, Wind Gate?"

Jordan could almost feel Adams' breath on the back of his neck.

"When you answer a question you're supposed to stand. Seems to me that you need some practice standing to your feet!" Hard Rock dismissed the rest of the class. Then, aided by another officer, he proceeded to send Jordan through what seemed like an hour of standing and sitting exercises.

Later, after having walked out the effects of his exercises, Jordan returned to the barracks. He thought about Oscar Tate. Two days ago they went to lunch without Oscar. When they returned to the barracks his lockers were empty, his boots and shoes no longer lined up under his bunk, which was stripped of covers, sheets, and pillowcase. Only the mattress with the imprint of Oscar's big body remained. The area from which Oscar joked, needled, and taunted the other cadets was clean enough to give the impression that nobody had occupied it lately. As Hollis, Willie, and Claude shined their boots, Oscar's absence was made more noticeable by the somber atmosphere.

"Anybody visited Sue lately?" Jordan said. He could not tell by Willie's expression whether he had done so or not. He just knew that he wanted to see her. It would also give him the opportunity to see Terri.

"Not today," Willie said. "But I need to brighten up her day. Make her forget her pains." He put down his boots and followed Jordan.

Claude was close behind.

Hollis, still shining a boot, blocked their path. "The medical people can take care of her."

65

Willie and Claude stopped as though Hollis was an officer. Hollis' entire demeanor was certainly not one of playfulness.

Jordan felt irritation rising within. He paused but was determined to challenge Hollis, boxing champion or no boxing champion.

"I don't give a damn about who's taking care of her," he said. Hollis moved directly in front of him blocking his path to the door like some immovable bronze statue. Jordan shifted to his left attempting to get past. But Hollis would not be moved. "You hard-headed fool!" Hollis dropped his boot and brush and assumed the stance of the college welterweight champion. "You're determined to destroy our chances before we get started!"

Jordan was so frustrated that he was willing to take his chances with Hollis. Balling up his fists, he took a stance that was clearly that of a neophyte.

Hollis' expression was one of puzzlement as though he just realized what he was doing. He dropped his guard. His expression softened as he searched for words of apology.

Jordan brushed past him out into the airfield, furious, completely fed up with the nearly unending confrontation he had with the officers, the policemen in Montgomery, and with Hollis Boyd. His jaw set, he walked briskly toward the telephone booth located next to the commissary, fighting back tears of anger. *To hell with this he thought. I was a darn good pilot at Velma Greer's Flying Academy without having to put up with anything close to the mess I have to put up with here!*

Overhead, black storm clouds were moving together. After a dry period longer than any previous one since he arrived, there would be rain. Fine, he thought. *I came here in a downpour. Why not leave in the same conditions?* He could see from a distance that the telephone booth was occupied. Just before he reached it the cadet hung up, nodded and left. This was it. No matter what his sister, father, and others would say when he arrived back in Columbus, he knew that he had no alternative but to get out of here. But they would make a big thing out of his return. They'd call him a quitter. They just did not know.

Inside the booth he stared at the phone, then at the telephone directory, then back at the telephone. Feeling hot tears cascading down his cheeks, stifling a sob, he grabbed the thin telephone directory, ripped it in half and flung it out of the booth into the airfield.

Slide Rice appeared as though on cue. "That make you feel better?" he drawled.

Jordan felt a flood of relief course through his entire being. "Sure in hell does!" He joined Slide in one good bend-at-the-waist-and-holding-their-sides laugh. They retrieved the two halves of the telephone book and stuck them back into the booth.

"Still lettin' white folks make you mad," Slide said matter-of-factly. He looked up at the clouds. He began dipping his paintbrushes into a can of gasoline and then wiping them off.

"I remember what you said about getting along with them, but… "

Slide chuckled. "I s'pect they're just doing the job they're s'pose to do." He finished cleaning the brushes and ambled toward a rickety, weather beaten truck filled with tools, equipment, and trash.

Jordan picked up Slide's ladder and followed him to the truck. "The problem is one of the cadets is nearly as bad as they are," he said.

Slide's truck might have been junky, but by the time he rearranged the tools and equipment and stacked empty boxes, cans, rags, broken pieces of wood and bricks into a corner, the truck bed had an appearance of orderliness. "Guess it just goes to show that deep down in a man's soul you won't see black or white."

Jordan was having a change of mind about Slide. Prior to now he considered him a typical lackey for the white man, a head-scratching darky who did not have one thought of his own about his own life. Sure he could work with his hands. But so what? His philosophy about how to survive was not totally acceptable.

Slide slammed shut the gate to the truck bed. "Just like the Book says. The good Lord created all of us alike."

The sign on the door that read Walter Rice, Inc., caught Jordan's attention. "You been running your own business for long?"

Slide opened the door and said in a voice filled with pride, "Near 'bout thirty-five years."

"That's a long time to be doing anything."

"Let's me take care of a wife and six young-uns. Or is it seven?" He laughed. The truck squeaked as he climbed in and slammed the door shut twice to make sure it would stay. Then he nodded toward the telephone booth. "You run all the way to the phone just to tear up the book? "

Jordan laughed. "No, but it made me feel a lot better."

Slide smiled, started the motor, and gave it some throttle to stop the coughing. Then he patted the gas pedal. "You know, I'm glad you smart young fellas are here. Gives me a chance to watch you fly Uncle Sam's planes."

Jordan watched the truck rumble away until it was out of sight.

CHAPTER SIX

Colonel Saunders was contemplating the meeting he had scheduled for the following Sunday morning. Captains Adams and Kanapka would be joining him soon, but until then he indulged in his morning ritual. He lingered over his usual breakfast of three eggs over easy, grits, two generous slices of ham, four biscuits, and coffee. His second wife, Ethel, whose appearance was as striking for its angularity as Buford's was for its girth, brought him the morning newspaper just as she had done for the ten years they had been married, which was just as his first wife had done for twenty years prior to her early death from tuberculosis. Ethel also delivered his wooden box full of cigars. As always, he took his time making his selection, picking up several of the long black cigars, sniffing and testing each one for compactness before deciding which one was absolutely right.

Ethel patted his head, kissed him on the cheek and left him to be by himself prior to his meeting. The morning air was fresh after a night of rain. Minnie, the Negro maid entered and gathered his dishes onto a tray. When Buford left Washington to assume command of the 99th, he and Ethel thought about bringing their maid from Washington, but the woman had balked at returning to the Deep South. As a result, they had to rely on Slide Rice's recommendation about Minnie. She proved to be every bit as efficient as the previous maid.

He watched Minnie walk away, the cheeks of her wide, full bottom bouncing with each step. She was heavier than the previous maid, but much prettier and definitely more cheerful. He never before enjoyed the luxury of two women catering to him so completely.

Buford felt comfortable around Minnie. She did her work willingly, talked when she was spoken to, and she knew how to cater to his needs almost before he knew what they were. She returned with the pot brimming with freshly made coffee, poured him a cup, sat the pot down, and left.

Why can't the cadets be like her? Or like the maid he left in Washington? Why can't they be like Slide Rice, who ran a business, but still realized where a good percentage of his business came from? 'Nigras' certainly didn't have enough money to make his business successful.

Buford called the meeting for two reasons. The first was to talk about 'Nigras' in particular, or "Negroes," as the smartass boys up North called them. 'Nigras' who arrived from the North, from the Midwest, and from the far West, places like California and Washington were a different breed. He noticed this difference when he encountered them in restaurants and other public facilities, indeed, wherever he came in contact with them. These 'Nigras' talked as well as he did. They could count, read, and write. They knew when to be quiet and when to study. And they had completed basic training in good shape. Of course basic training was easy for them. *Everyone knows that 'Nigras' are athletically inclined, but successfully completing a physically taxing obstacle course was not flying a plane.*

Hard Rock Adams was the first officer to arrive. For as long as Buford had known Adams, including having him under his command, he could not remember him ever being late. Instead, like now, he arrived earlier than was necessary, before Buford was ready for him. Buford thought highly of punctuality but he was not in favor of extremism in any way.

The second concern on Buford's agenda was the matter of Adolf Hitler. The newspaper headlines indicated that the chances of the United States entering the war in Europe were increasing daily. Hitler seemed hell-bent on destruction until Germany ruled all of Europe. And after that who knew how much farther he would go? The man was a maniac. His

70

Luftwaffe was devastating. And if President Roosevelt did declare war, only America's best soldiers and marines could stop him on the ground. Only the best fighter pilots could defeat the Luftwaffe.

Adams returned from making a telephone call, smiling proudly, a smile, incidentally, that the cadets never saw. Now he sat across from Buford, refused a cigar, preferring instead to smoke a Lucky Strike cigarette.

"Well, Captain, when in the past I've seen that grin it usually meant good news from a lady friend."

"Just a clerical worker at the camp." Adams started to pour himself a cup of coffee, but instead allowed Minnie to do so. He added just a drop of cream.

"I suppose you have been here long enough to have bedded down a clerical worker or two. Perhaps in your office?"

Adams turned on a look of innocence. "Business, sir, business. Marge tells me that the next class of wouldbe fighter pilots won't be as big as the current one."

Buford laughed. "If they keep getting smaller, this experiment will die sooner than I thought."

"That's hard to believe, sir."

"Well, nearly. I don't know for sure whether that maniac overseas will force us into this war. But if he does... I'd like to think that I could feel safe back here."

Minnie entered, followed by Captain Kanapka.

"All right," Buford said. "We're ready to start. I know that I haven't called the two of you here on a Sunday morning before. Before now I haven't seen anything so serious that couldn't be taken care of in five days. No more than six. And certainly nothing that couldn't be taken care of in the line of duty."

Minnie brought a platter of steaming scrambled eggs,

71

bacon, and biscuits.

"I do hope you men haven't eaten yet. After eating army chow I guarantee that you'll appreciate Minnie's magic in the kitchen. Nobody can do what she does with a bag of groceries. But her breakfast is extra special."

She grinned self-consciously and hurried away. But Buford knew that she appreciated his bragging on her. He buttered a biscuit. "I think I've made it pretty clear from the beginning the doubts I have about this, this 'experiment.' I'll probably never get another chance to go to war, but if we do, I'd like to get in my bed confident that I'll wake up the next morning. And having done that, to know that I won't be confined to my house or running for my life. Or about to be hauled off to a prison camp in my own country."

"That being the case, Hard Rock has just received some encouraging news."

"That's right," said Adams. "The next cadet class will be smaller than the previous ones."

Buford gobbled down the second half of a biscuit, belched loudly, and patted his big stomach. "It's going like I predicted. Those inflated IQ's running Washington think that they know everything. Hell, some of them came from places where they never saw a 'Nigra'. But, I've been around them since I was knee-high to a grasshopper."

"Sir, you do know that each of the cadets has a college degree?" said Kanapka.

Adams chuckled. "Does having a college degree guarantee that a man can fly a plane?"

"Good question, Good question, indeed." Buford, having eaten all that he could hold, now picked up his cigar. He started to relight it, but taking into consideration that Adams and Kanapka were still eating, simply stuck it into his mouth and rolled it from one side to the other. "Our research tells me most of them graduated from 'Nigra' colleges. Need I say more? I've said all along it will fail. And the closer we get to going to war the more sure I am that I'm right."

"Sir," said Adams, "are we really getting close to going to war?"

"Damn close, Captain. Damn close. I'll be the most surprised one here if any of the cadets in the current class manages to solo."

Kanapka finished eating, placed his silverware neatly onto his plate and wiped his mouth. "There have been some cadets in each of the previous classes that have made it through."

"A handful, Captain. Just a handful. We'll be here forever engaged in what could only be called a futile endeavor. Futile, men! That's the most appropriate word I can think of."

Kanapka said, "There are at least two cadets that will make it through this class, sir. Cadet Boyd and Cadet Wingate. Possibly others. But those two for sure."

Adams laughed. "Those two, maybe. Sir, an interesting situation has developed. We've made Boyd the leader. Unofficially, I mean, but still the leader. Yet, Wingate is much more popular with the cadets."

"What are you saying?" Buford lit his cigar. "I know that you have some plan in that devious mind of yours."

"Competition, sir. Friendly competition never hurt any group of military men, I don't care what color they are."

"All right, let's hear it."

"Sir, we should let Wingate solo first."

Buford thought about that for a few seconds. "If your assessment of their preference for Wingate is right then all the cadets will be happy. So what's the point?"

"But Boyd's got a great deal of pride. I see it in him just like in some of us."

73

Kanapka said, "Don't you see it in Wingate?'

"Wingate's a damn goof off!" Adams responded a little too strongly. "A show-off. A wise-ass!"

"All right. All right, men!" Saunders said obviously enjoying this conflict. "Continue with your plan, Adams."

"Sir, the men like Wingate. But based on the fact we've designated Boyd as the leader they expect him to solo first."

"Even though Wingate has a little more distinguished background flying?" Kanapka obviously did not appreciate Adams' reasoning.

"Wingate's flying experience was as a civilian," said Adams. "Boyd's was in connection with the college he went to. But all that's beside the point."

"Captain, let me see if I understand your reasoning," Buford said. "You think that by scheduling Wingate to solo first, we would create enough animosity between the two leading cadets to cause the death knell of this class?"

"Sir, we all know that a little competition never hurt any group of military men."

Kanapka said, "Sir, don't you think for the morale of the unit it would be better for the one in the leadership position to go first?'

"Seems to me that the morale might be higher if any one of them managed to solo," Adams said. "To tell you the truth I'm not so sure that either of them can."

"Sir?" Kanapka forced himself to tolerate Adams.

Saunders puffed on his cigar a few times, removed it from his mouth and examined it. "Captain Adams, you're the officer in charge of this phase of training. I'll depend on you to make the right decision."

Adams grinned at Kanapka. "Yes, sir!"

After the captains left, Buford lingered. He knew that Captain Lloyd Kanapka thought differently about the 'Nigra' cadets than did any of the other officers. That was never more evident than in the talk they just had.

He remembered the friction that surfaced between Kanapka and Adams the first meeting he held months ago. Then he hoped that his staff would come to be on one accord. In the past he was known as an officer's favorite leader. During his twenty-five years in the United States Army, most of them in leadership roles, he gained a reputation for allowing those officers in his command to make suggestions. Unlike some commanding officers who led by intimidation, he encouraged feedback even then. He might have been the target of those who contended that he was arrogant and a little too much of a showboat, but they could never say that he didn't care about his junior officers. His reputation was such that he never had problems pulling together a strong, efficient staff for his assignments, whether in the United States or in Europe.

But something about Lloyd Kanapka was different. Something seemed to be bothering him during their meetings. He only joined them during after-hour gatherings in the officer's club when his presence was mandatory. After an early confrontation between the two officers, he knew that he would have to meet with Kanapka. The time was at hand. It turned out that he would not have to wait too long.

"Buford. Captain Kanapka is still here," Ethel said.

Kanapka entered, apologized for wanting to take up more of his time, but Buford was glad that he had stayed. Kanapka refused a drink, but accepted his offer to move into the living room to a more relaxed setting.

"I can't say I'm totally surprised that you're back, Captain. I know that you've had some major differences of opinion with Captain Adams from the beginning." He observed Kanapka's reactions to see how close he was to being right. "And I must say that I've not noticed a change for the better

75

over these months. A matter of considerable concern. I am totally aware of the records of both you and Captain Adams."

Kanapka sat very still and relaxed during his speech. One of the characteristics Saunders admired about this officer from the beginning was his coolness, his ability to remain unperturbed regardless of what was going on around him.

"Sir, did you know my father?"

"Not well," Buford responded. "I never served with him, but from what I've heard he was a fine officer."

"We had a few differences."

"How so?" Buford was genuinely interested in Kanapka's answer.

"Well, he was a product of the South. I was born and spent much of my childhood in the North. Our relationship with Negroes was somewhat different…"

"You know that I was born and raised down here!" Buford arose. He needed to stretch, and he was much better at handling conflict on his feet.

"Yes, sir. May I go on?"

"By all means."

"Sir, other than the difference in our attitudes about Negroes, I am pretty much the product of my father. I remember most of his commands during his career. At least eight. He believed very strongly in total dedication to making whatever unit he commanded the best."

"Admirable goal. I think any commanding officer worth his salt should be totally dedicated."

"Glad to know you feel that way, sir. To tell you the truth, knowing that you would be the commanding officer here is one of the reasons I applied for this assignment."

"I see. Well, at times I've wondered. I can't find fault with your performance, but at times your attitude has bothered me. Now I realize what's been bothering you."

Minnie appeared to make sure that everything was all right and that they were comfortable, then left.

"Tell me, son, did your father ever have an assignment like this one?"

"No, sir. Of course no one else has either. We know that this is a special assignment."

"Experiment." Saunders arose, breathing heavily. "An experiment doomed to failure. And everybody knows it's doomed except a few liberal intellectuals in Washington and the handful of cadets here now and another handful on the way."

"Sir," Kanapka arose, "count me in with the few believers."

Buford sighed, shook his head in acknowledgment. His admiration for Kanapka, based on his optimism about the success of this proposed Negro fighter squadron was tempered by his own thinking that it would not work.

"Sir," Kanapka had reached the door on his way out when he turned to face Buford. "May I ask you at what point you started doubting that this program would succeed?"

"A better question to ask is if I ever believed that it would."

Kanapka's expression was one of bafflement.

"I know you want to know how that can be so when my history shows that I never accepted a command I didn't have the greatest amount of faith in, that I didn't fully expect to be a crack outfit that would succeed in peacetime and during wartime. The difference here for this experiment is that my acceptance was not a choice. It was an order. And whereas in any previous assignments where I had no choice, I always reached the point where I changed my opinion about my outfit. But this is a different story."

"Well sir," Kanapka said, "perhaps there is still time for you to change your mind about the Tuskegee Airmen."

77

"They'd have to show me that they warrant being called airmen, Captain."

"I'm sure they will, sir." Kanapka saluted and left.

Buford watched the entrance from which Kanapka departed as if expecting him to return one more time. If he had any doubts about Kanapka's intentions, he didn't any more. Neither did he have any doubts about his intensity. Yet intensity was one thing, and belief in an individual or group to perform was another. He would monitor the performance of this class, especially Wingate and Boyd, very closely in the future. However, as far as he was concerned, Kanapka was just another one of those crazy Northern fools trying to do something that everyone else knew better than to do; put 'Nigras' in the same category as white people. He was more convinced than ever this program was a waste of time and money. And it was just a matter of time before the smart boys in Washington realized that he had been right all along.

CHAPTER SEVEN

On a sultry summer midmorning at Tuskegee Airfield, Jordan along with the other cadets, listened to Hard Rock Adams explain the various features of the BT-13 trainer airplane. Until recently, the classes on aircraft identification were held in a large classroom. Identification had been relegated to enlarged photographs of airplanes featuring each part in detail. However, just as Hard Rock assured them time after time during the training classes, diagrams, pictures, or even mock airplanes could not compare with the real thing.

"Now pay close attention," Adams said. "We've had a few cases of engine trouble with these little bastards." He paused in front of Claude, smiling as he placed particular emphasis on engine trouble. "No need to piss in your pants, but if your plane develops engine trouble, any fancy turns could damn well be your last!"

The silence that existed during Adams' dramatic presentation disturbed Jordan. By now he had been around Adams long enough to determine when his intentions were to intimidate rather than to train. He noticed Captain Kanapka and Colonel Saunders walking toward them. "How long before we start flying, sir?" he said.

Adams stopped, wheeled around and fixed one of his baleful stares on Jordan. "What's that, Wind Gate?"

"When do we go up, sir?"

"Well, since we don't want you killing yourself right away, not for at least a day!"

One of the officers laughed. Other than that, silence reigned. As they took turns following Adams and the other officers inside the plane, Jordan noticed Hollis frowning at him.

During the next two hours, each of them sat in the

79

rear cockpit of the trainer while Hard Rock or one of the other officers flew. The wind was nearly nonexistent so the ride was smooth.

Afterward, Adams gave them a ten-minute break and called the other officers for a conference. Colonel Saunders and Captain Kanapka joined the group.

Jordan thought this phase of the training was boring. Identifying various parts of a plane was not nearly as fulfilling as actually flying. Neither was sitting in classes listening to Adams or one of the other officers lecture for 45-minute periods on subjects like precision, aeronautics, formation, and instruments. He wasn't sure how long he could endure this preliminary flight training. He knew that part of his boredom stemmed from his background. Some of the others had flight training, but in conversations with them, he learned that none of them equaled his number of flight hours.

"All right, Wind Gate!" Adams called out. "You're such an eager beaver. Let's go!"

Jordan overcame his surprise, bouncing up as if he expected to be given this opportunity. Aware of the other cadets watching him, he followed Hard Rock to the airplane.

"This is your show." Adams nodded toward the cockpit. Jordan obliged. Hard Rock climbed into the trainee seat behind him. They strapped themselves into their seats.

"All right, let's see what in hell you can do!"

Jordan guided the BT-13 down the runway, lifted it off the ground as smoothly as any veteran pilot, climbed to conservative height, and leveled it off. With Adams accompanying him, he knew better than to try any risky maneuvers. Conservative flying was the key. He flew steadily, never varying that level more than a few feet.

"All right," Adams shouted. "Let's take her down!"

Jordan banked the plane sharply and descended to the

airfield. The plane bounced twice before stopping. Though the cadets were too intimidated to applaud, their verbal responses said it all. He heard cries of, "Attaboy, Cadet," and "You showed 'em, Hotshot!" Jordan strolled toward them, winking and giving his customary thumbs-up sign.

Adams shouted, "Wind Gate, you want to show off, go join a carnival!" Then he moved closer, peering into Jordan's eyes, nearly on the tips of his toes, "You want to kill your fool self, do it when you're flying alone. You understand?"

"Yes, sir!" Jordan knew that he had done nothing to warrant the verbal abuse, but he was so accustomed to this kind of response from Adams he was not sure he would know how to react to civility from him. The looks he received from most of the other cadets were reassuring. He could tell that they appreciated his flying skills. Everyone, that is, but Hollis Boyd, whose expression bordered on contempt.

Jordan decided that two weeks with no word about Oscar's disappearance was too much. Queries by Willie and Claude produced unsatisfactory answers as to his whereabouts. As far as any of the cadets were concerned, Oscar had simply disappeared. Jordan knew that none of the cadets had questioned Hard Rock or any other officer working with them during this phase of flight training. He decided to ask Kanapka. For two days, he prepared himself to make an appointment with the captain. Finally he was ready to take his chances on getting a satisfactory answer, being completely ignored, or, as Willie warned, being made to dig another six by six foot hole.

"I think your best bet right now is to say and do what you're asked to say and do," Claude said.

Willie agreed. "It's like this, Hotshot. We don't know

81

what happened to Oscar. But we do know we sure can't afford to lose you. Next thing you know the wheels will cancel this class for not enough participation. That's all I need if I want to hear folks back in California poke fun at me for the rest of my life."

Everyone else agreed. If Jordan would just lead by example, everything would be all right. Claude and Willie assured him that he was not aware of the esteem in which he was held by some of the other cadets.

What he was not sure of was how much he liked the emphasis Claude, Willie, and others were placing on his importance. True, he wanted to become a fighter pilot. The desire to do so burned within him, an inferno that got increasingly hotter. He had not felt a desire this intense since he was a high school football star expecting to continue his success in college. He had been comfortable being a star, running the ball, following his blockers until he saw enough daylight to escape tacklers trying to stop his progress. He was comfortable here at Tuskegee being the star pilot responsible only for himself. As he dressed to attend the new night club for cadets, he thought if he only had to keep his own house clean, how much easier it would be for him to get through this training and to one day be an ace fighter pilot.

The hospital at Tuskegee Airfield had been completed. It was one of a continuous number of facilities being constructed as class after class of cadets arrived for training. The ongoing construction was a testimony to the haste in which the United States Army Air Corps tried to adhere to President Roosevelt's signing of the executive order. It was a testimony to the lack of preparedness of the Department of War. But as some of the cadets admitted, at least the government was making accommodations.

Sue greeted Jordan, Willie, and Terri wearing a small

bandage on her forehead. The absence of all other evidence of the accident was miraculous, considering the number and the severity of the bruises she bore just a short time ago. When Willie tried to hug her, she flinched.

"Willie, boy, it's not that I don't crave the feel of your manly arms, it's just that my body can't stand it. Just the thought is painful," she said.

"Okay, Brown Sugar," he said. "I'll accept that excuse for right now."

Jordan said, "Sue, you look just as good as you did when we met."

"Terri, honey," she said, "did you know this flyboy knows how to lie real smooth-like?"

As they walked to the club, Sue said, "Jordan, boy I heard that you've gotten real serious about seeing this thing through."

Jordan nodded.

"Maybe you ought to clear that with Hard Rock," Willie said. "None of us are too sure whether he plans to let Jordan graduate."

"What about you, Sue? After what happened," Jordan said.

"Didn't Terri tell you how tough I am? Real mean, too. Takes more than a Southern policeman to make me quit."

Her voice was filled with such a degree of resolve that Jordan and the others had no reason to doubt her.

"Tell me, has Mr. Claude McCall joined Oscar Tate, wherever he is?"

Willie laughed. "Book Man? He's probably at the library with all the other readers. I think he opens it in the morning and closes it at night."

Inside, the new club was nothing flashy. Drab brown and beige paneling covered the walls of the room that seated a hundred people comfortably. The floor was hardwood. The lights were dimmer in the seating area than they were in the dancing area. At 8:00, a five-piece band began heating up what had been a cool atmosphere. Jordan wasted no time asking Terri to dance. It seemed to him that it had been too long. Just being able to let himself go and keep in step to the lively music was a great relief. It was liberating, allowing him to break through the walls of confinement and be free to move his body any way he wanted to. It was a release from the bondage of Hard Rock Adams, the tormentor who relished keeping him there. He vowed not to even think of anything beyond the four walls of the club.

He saw Willie dancing with a young woman whose movements hinted of Sue's. Whenever Willie caught Jordan's eye, he flashed a smile and made a fancy move. Jordan pretended not to see him. Because of Jordan's lack of attention, plus the limited capability of his partner to keep up with him, Willie soon cut out the exhibition. Two times he appealed to Sue, but she preferred to remain a spectator. Considering the enjoyment she got from dancing, Jordan knew she must still be in pain.

In the midst of an upbeat number, Jordan saw Oscar Tate, dressed in civilian clothes, enter and stand by a table close to the entrance. The dance ended for Terri, Willie, and himself. Drawn by Oscar's broad, magnetic smile they rushed over to the table.

"I couldn't believe it was you," Jordan said pumping Oscar's hand.

Oscar would not settle with just a handshake. He pulled, literally yanked, Jordan into an embrace. He did the same with Willie and Terri.

"Looks like the mystery is about to be solved." Willie pretended to be massaging the pain from his arms. "Pork-Chop, where in hell did you disappear to?"

Before Oscar began his explanation, Sue whispered something to Terri and excused herself.

"Hey, Oscar," said Jordan, "has anybody told you you're in flight training?"

The other cadets agreed.

Oscar held up his hands to quiet them. "All of you lightweight Negroes are in flight training." He took a big swig of beer, belched, and patted his belly, which appeared to protrude more than it had the last time any of them had seen him. "Old Pork Chop is too heavy in the gut and in the posterior, or to be more to the point, in the ass, to be a fighter pilot. At least that's what Hard Rock told me."

Other cadets moved around the table. They apparently had missed Oscar as much as Jordan and Willie did.

"Hell of a time to tell you!" Jordan said. He felt anger rising within.

"Ain't it the truth now." Oscar stood up as more cadets gathered. "When they told me, I decided right then and there to pack my bags. Even though they offered me the opportunity to stay here as a mechanic, I said to hell with them and their project." He took another swig of beer. "All the years I had spent dreaming about flying — ever since Lindbergh's flight."

"That's right!" Willie said.

A chorus of agreement emanated from the other cadets as the atmosphere began to look and sound like a Baptist church during a Sunday morning worship service.

Oscar continued, "I remember hearing about how my country was gonna give me a chance to fly, but then to be told we're limiting you spooks to one type of pilot."

"Damn shame!" One of the cadets shouted. That sparked a loud chorus of similar responses.

Oscar rapidly warmed up to the attention he was getting. Now that the band had quit playing, the musicians

85

joined Oscar's audience. "So I asked myself, what's the use? I've lost again. Just another dream wrecked."

"No. Not this time!" Jordan assured him.

"That's right, Hotshot! I said, wait just a minute, O.T. We're a first. We're an original bunch of Negroes. The cream of the crop getting together to defend our country! That's right, our country!"

"Go ahead, Poke Chops!" Willie shouted.

Oscar seemed to be soaring into some other world. "This is a team effort if there ever was one! Pilots can't fight if the planes don't get in the air!"

"Or if they don't stay up there!" said a chorus of voices.

"That's right. I said, O.T., you're a damned good mechanic!" He leaned forward, cupped his hand over his mouth as if revealing some well-kept secret. "And everybody knows they're gonna need some damned good mechanics to keep those cans they call airplanes in the air!"

Jordan and every other cadet there knew what Oscar meant. They greeted his "revelation" with laughter.

"But you know what?" He continued in his same confidential posture, "I'd stay here with you cats even if I had to scrape pots or clean toilet bowls seven days a week!"

By then, the cadets were in a state of near frenzy. Jordan, followed by others, rushed toward Oscar to shake his hand and to embrace him, but he was not finished. He pulled away from a cadet who was hugging him most energetically. The noise decreased as the cadets strained to hear what else this fiery orator had to say.

"You know what? It's just a damned great feeling being part of this team!"

Later, outside the two room apartment Terri shared with Sue, she told Jordan not to enter until she gave the "all clear" signal. But he entered before she'd given the signal, laughing as she jammed a flimsy undergarment under a pillow.

"Instant maid service," he said, pulling her to him and kissing her.

"Hold on, Cadet." She pulled away gently but determined.

"Why, sugar? I've wanted to do that for a long, long time." He pulled her close again.

She remained in his arms but leaned away. "Is that all?"

Jordan was somewhat puzzled. "What do you mean?"

She laughed huskily. "I mean what happens after a kiss or two?" She surprised him by kissing him passionately. Her softness, the fragrance of her perfume, her aggressiveness had a mesmerizing effect.

He broke the kiss. "I don't get serious with women," he said more abruptly than he intended.

She laughed, "Take them lightly. Is that the Wingate style?"

"That's right. That's my style."

She pressed against him putting her arms around his neck. "No commitments to anything or anybody. Especially women. Right?"

He pulled her to him hungrily covering her mouth with his. Then they were undressing each other frantically as though making up for lost time.

Afterward Terri purred, "Too bad there's no restaurant to get something to eat. Then we could come back and try this again."

"Hold on, girl. Hold on." He was buttoning his shirt.

"That's right, Jordan "Loverboy" Wingate doesn't want to get tied down to one woman." She crawled across the bed behind him, flung her arms around his waist and kissed him on

87

the neck.

He pulled her onto his lap, kissed her passionately and released her. He knew she could tell that his mind was on something else. He moved from the bed and sat in a comfortable wooden chair. She brought him a glass of water, put on her robe, and waited for him to talk.

"To get through this phase of training we have to solo. Fly alone... I could do that tomorrow. Could have done it the first day."

" I know. Because you told me you could. So did Willie. So?"

"I have this strange feeling about our leaders. I've heard about the harassment recruits get in the military. It's one of the aspects of training that you expect even though you might not like it. But our leaders," each time he said the word he knew that it came out sarcastically. "The harassment is supposed to help you they say. Say it sharpens your reflexes, toughens you up, and helps you to be more obedient to the officers during the dangers of war." He handed her his empty beer glass.

"Well," she poured him another glassful. "Are you complaining about that? I mean don't you want to be alert if people are shooting at you? If we got involved?"

Jordan said, "Everybody's pretty sure we'll get into the war. The question is when. If Hard Rock Adams doesn't kick most of us out and kill the rest of us through our training, we should get our chance to fight." He thought about this. "Hard to believe, but the longer I'm here the more I suspect that our leaders have as many, if not more, doubts about us than civilians and the wheels in D.C." He drank half of his second glass of beer.

Terri's expression was a mixture of doubts and fear. "So where do you go from here? Who can you complain to?"

"I think the answer to that is nobody." He knew that was

the answer. "We have to pull together as a team. The cadets I mean. That's the only way."

She looked surprised.

"I know how strange it sounds hearing me talk about a team effort. But I think that's the only way we can win. That's the only way we'll get a chance to show what we're made of." He kissed her and left.

On the airfield, on a terribly hot day, Hard Rock Adams was chewing out Claude for banking the plane too vigorously on the turns. Today, the captain was outdoing himself in the art of verbal abuse. Not only did he use more profanity and spit out his words more vigorously than before, but his tirades lasted longer. Today, no cadet who flew was exempt from his tirades. Today, a "Hard Rock" hit each cadet who flew.

"Mr. Dumb-ass, where in hell have you been during classes?" Adams shouted at Claude.

"Here, sir! I mean there!" This was a typical response from Claude. Jordan had been embarrassed numerous times by Claude's nearly petrifying fear whenever Adams confronted him. The man who was so cool, low-keyed, and sure of himself continued to act like a frightened child under Adams' verbal attack.

"Did one of my instructors teach you to open the damned throttle as far as you could on turns? If so, I want you to point him out to me! The problem with you niggers is you don't have a hint of coordination! Not a hint!"

Saunders, followed by Kanapka, approached them at a brisk pace, their faces showing that they had brought serious news.

"It's just been announced that we're in a state of war against the Japanese, the Germans, and the Italians!" Saunders bellowed. "Are you boys ready to risk your lives for your country or piss away your time here?" Behind thick glasses his

89

eyes twinkled as they traveled from the face of one cadet and then another. Then he exchanged salutes with the officers and departed followed by Kanapka.

Adams, waiting until they were out of sight added, "Any of you have balls enough to learn how to lay your asses on the line for America? Probably not," he chuckled. "While white men are somewhere protecting your asses, you'll be at home sucking on your mammies tits!"

Jordan looked into Adams' eyes and held his gaze.

Adams frown changed to defiance. He laughed without smiling. "Dismissed, girls."

Jordan paused, attempting to maintain eye contact with Adams to communicate that he disagreed without speaking. Adams broke the contact and started to walk away. Jordan lingered to see whether he would look back. He didn't, so Jordan turned to leave.

"Wind Gate!"

Jordan turned and saw the cocky captain marching toward him. "Attention! I ought to order you to stand in this position for the rest of your damned life." He didn't move as close to Jordan as he usually did. "I want you to know that remark was aimed at you specifically. None of these cadets is more of a tit-sucker than you!" He turned and departed in the same manner. "At ease," he called from a distance. "Dismissed!"

Jordan entered the barracks. The atmosphere was tense and still. Obviously, the news about war had affected them. Willie sat on his footlocker, going through the motions of shining a boot. Claude sat on his trying to write a letter. He rose and crossed over to the window, frowned, then pushed himself to write another word or two. Several of the cadets lay on their bunks, eyes closed or staring into space. Hollis was not there.

Jordan let himself be immersed in the tomb-like silence

for a time, a short time. "Hey, Claude," he said, walking toward the scholarly one, "you sure you're coordinated enough to write that letter?" Receiving nothing more than a grunt he decided to continue. He stood over Claude and peered down at the letter. "I mean how in heck do you expect to fly one of Uncle Sam's big old airplanes if your fingers are too clumsy to write?"

"Wind Gate," Claude said.

"Jordan's right," said Willie. "Like Hard Rock said, better develop you some hand-to-eye coordination before you even think about flying one of his planes."

The other cadets came alive and drifted into Claude's area. Claude smiled. "That's right. I don't care how much dancing and ball playing you colored boys can do. I still say you're uncoordinated."

Though most of the cadets tried to imitate Hard Rock, Claude had become the master.

Jordan said, "That's right, in things that really matter. We'll show them how much coordination we have when we graduate from here, cum laude I might add."

Willie stared at Jordan with a mock serious expression. "Cum what? Boy, where'd you learn how to say words like that?"

"Why, at a little ole Negro, no, at a little ole 'Nigra' college, sir."

The other cadets laughed uproariously.

"As I was saying," Jordan continued, "we will graduate from here and go overseas and kick Hitler's butt!"

"Damn right!" said Willie. "And another son of a bitch like him!"

The other cadets joined in changing the morgue-like atmosphere into one of jubilation.

Hollis entered and observed them from a distance. Silence returned.

Jordan said, "Are you ready to fight Hitler?"

Hollis shrugged. "I don't see how we can think about fighting anybody unless we graduate from here." He walked past them into the latrine.

"That cadet sure does know how to kill a party." Claude gathered his writing materials.

Jordan nodded. "In order to graduate you have to fly. The question is, can he do that?"

He only had to wait until the following morning to have his question answered. Hollis was scheduled to be the first cadet to go up. A few minutes past dawn, Hollis nonchalantly followed one of the instructors to a plane. The cadets watched the two of them climb into the cabins of a training plane, hesitate long enough for Hollis to make his checks, and to start the motor. Jordan noticed Claude's eyes on him as he watched Hollis guide the plane bumpily down the runway and lift off smoothly. Jordan had to admit to himself that things were so far so good for Hollis. When Hollis was a few feet above minimum flying height, he caught Claude looking at him again with a bit of a smirk. Later, when Hollis completed a few turns without losing control, Jordan glanced at Claude. When Hollis touched down hard, bumped, and rolled just a bit longer than Jordan thought that he should, he smiled and winked at Claude.

Later, Jordan finished shopping in the post exchange. Just outside he noticed that one of the two telephones was not being used. *Got to take advantage of this,* he thought. These were the only telephones available for the cadets to make long distance calls. *The parents will be shocked to hear me.*

"Jordan, boy!" Mose exclaimed.

Jordan could hear shouting in the background.

His mother cried, "Is this my boy?"

"It sure is. Good to hear your voices, Mama and Daddy."

"Well, glad you're still there, son. Your sister ain't here right now. You know she sure would want to hear your voice and all you've got to say."

"Tell Annie that everything's all right here. I plan to stick with it all the way. In fact it won't be too long before I solo. After that, it's just a matter of keeping my nose clean as they say here."

"Good to hear you say that, son," said his mother. "We're real proud of you."

Later, he felt much better having talked with them for just the second time since he left home. It strengthened his commitment to stay by verbalizing it to his family. As he walked to the barracks, he felt his inner resolve strengthen. The verbalization was not just a promise, but also a declaration for others. By the time he reached the barracks, his resolve to succeed, to shine, excited him so that he could hardly contain himself.

Inside the building, Willie, who had been playing solitaire, greeted him. "Seems like I can beat everybody but myself," he said. "All right, Hotshot, what's your reaction to the Bible Boy's flight today?"

Claude entered from the latrine.

Jordan smiled and shrugged his shoulders. "How am I supposed to answer that? You want me to say I wasn't impressed? Or that I can do better?"

"No reason to even doubt that." Willie painted a visual and verbal picture. "Hotshot Wingate takes off beautifully, executes all aspects of flying magnificently, turns and lands perfectly. And then he stro---"

"Who're you kidding," said Claude. "That's too easy for Jordan Wingate. There is no way that he can fly without exhibiting his flair for theatrics."

"Hey, Book Man, will you speak English?" Jordan

93

said.

"All right, Mr. Wingate. After the two of you solo, maybe someday we'll get the opportunity to witness the two of you in a contest."

"Come to Columbus," Jordan said. "The home of daredevil flying."

"I understand that Hollis is to be the first one to fly solo." Claude picked up the deck of cards. "Anybody want to bet against that happening?" He had his eyes on Willie despite the number of cadets in the barracks.

Willie, always ready to accept a challenge, eyed him with a fiendish gleam in his eyes. "Book Man, I do think I'll have to take some of that action." He looked over his shoulders to make sure there were no spies nearby. "These folks might be a little slow, but they know who the best pilot is. It's Hotshot."

The other cadets lined up on either Willie's or Claude's side. They were up to anything for some fun, anything to escape the continuous strain, compounded now by the announcement of war.

"I'm impressed with Hotshot's confidence," Claude said, "but I'm also aware of Hard Rock's rather strong, ah, feelings toward Jordan. I'll have to go with Hollis."

Jordan figured that Hollis soloing first was a foregone conclusion. They would want a good example leading off, a pacesetter. He knew that he was a better pilot, but two factors were clear-cut guarantees that Hollis would solo first. The first was Adams' preference toward Hollis as their leader, and the second was his obvious and instant dislike for Jordan. If Hollis flew solo first, everyone would know that he had been formally designated the leader of their class. Jordan dwelled on this probability, mulled it over in his mind. He fell asleep having accepted it.

Jordan was impressed by Colonel Saunders' office and its military pictures, plaques, and bric-a-brac. He could tell that the colonel was a proud man by the way he sat straight in his seat, his head erect, his shoulders squared, trying to mirror the much younger, leaner major in the giant oil painting. Saunders' presence captivated Jordan. He nearly forgot that Captain Adams and Captain Kanapka were in the room.

"Congratulations, Cadet Wingate," Saunders' eye contact with him was fleeting. "Must be quite an honor to be chosen to be the first cadet in your class to solo."

"Yes, sir!"

"At ease, Cadet Wingate." Saunders' eyes bounced around the room again before landing on his target. "Seems to be the overall consensus. Any questions, Cadet Wingate?"

"No, sir."

"Good. Good. Takeoff time at the crack of dawn, Captain Adams?"

"That's right, sir."

Outside Jordan took a deep breath. He really did have some questions about his leaders.

CHAPTER EIGHT

Jordan knew that Hard Rock Adams had two choices; either he or Hollis would solo first. In this, the advanced stage of flight training, none of the other cadets were ready. Willie was close. After a shaky start, he decided that being a rebel playboy interfered with training which could lead to an early dismissal, so he decided to get serious about the business of becoming a fighter pilot. Claude had made some progress. Lately, he seemed less intimidated, but he was not ready. The six other cadets in the class were at various stages of readiness.

Jordan thought more clearly when he walked. The breeze blowing was a welcome relief from the spell of sweltering days and hot nights. Clouds were forming overhead. He stuck a stick of spearmint gum in his mouth, chewing slowly, savoring the sweetness. He remembered Hard Rock Adam's response when Colonel Saunders told him that he would be the first in his class to solo. The captain had not gushed with ' happiness. That would have been out of character. But his smile had been wide enough to show that he was in total agreement. Captain Kanapka responded differently, frowning slightly, but otherwise remaining passive. Jordan suspected that he disagreed with the others, but he needed to make certain.

That evening, after weighing the pros and cons of the situation, he dressed in a clean pair of fatigues, shined his boots, especially the hard toe, then walked hurriedly, and he hoped inconspicuously, to the post phone booth. He was relieved to see a new directory. Having located Captain Kanapka's address, he hurried on to his house. Mrs. Kanapka, speaking in a Midwestern accent, informed him that her husband was working at his office. Jordan thanked her and jogged toward the administration building. He was in luck. The captain was there.

Captain Kanapka's office was furnished rather austerely with a wooden chair, a desk, a clock, and two pictures, one of the captain and his wife, and another of two young teenage boys.

"At ease, Cadet Wingate." The captain's voice was surprisingly soft, and its warmth transcended the cold plainness of the room. "What can I do for you?"

"Sir, I don't think . . . I don't think I can keep my appointment tomorrow morning."

"Your appointment?" Kanapka's quizzical expression masked a smile. He waited for Jordan to continue.

"To solo, sir."

Kanapka cleared his throat, tapped a forefinger on his desk, "Why is that, Cadet Wingate?"

"Well, sir, I've got this terrible stomachache. I think it's called a nervous stomach. Sometimes, the night before I'm supposed to do something real important my stomach gets so upset I can't do anything."

"I see," said Kanapka. "And do you think this nervous stomach might get worse by tomorrow morning?"

In spite of the serious tone of Kanapka's voice and his attempt to look surprised, Jordan sensed that the captain was on to his plan and that he approved.

"And that it might get worse until Cadet Boyd solos first."

"Yes, sir." He felt more comfortable knowing that Kanapka knew. "Sir, I didn't know whether to talk to you, Captain Adams, or the colonel."

"Oh, you came to the right officer all right. I'll handle it from here."

"Thank you, sir, " Jordan said exchanging salutes with the captain.

"And by the way, Cadet Wingate, do be sure to take care

of that terrible nervous stomach."

"Yes, sir." Outside he walked toward the barracks, relieved to have done something totally foreign to him, refusing an opportunity to compete.

Early the next morning, he observed the other cadets and officers at the flight line watching Hollis stride toward the plane. Boyd smiled confidently before climbing into the cockpit. This time no officer climbed in with him.

Jordan felt a tinge of jealousy and regret that he had made the sacrifice. But, just as quickly, he felt satisfied with the thought that if he and Hollis were to be important cogs in the wheel of the 99th Pursuit Squadron, the first group of Negro fighter pilots, they were going to have to get along better.

Afterwards, Jordan entered a conference room, where Hollis, having successfully completed his solo, was standing in the front with Adams, Kanapka, and other officers. Hollis was wearing his dress summer khakis with a tie.

"Cadet Boyd," Adams said, moving toward Hollis carrying a pair of scissors. He reached up and grabbed Hollis' tie as though he were going to strangle him. "It gives me great pleasure to uphold an Air Corps tradition." He snipped the tie in half. "Congratulations on being the first cadet in your class to solo." Adams' voice was full of sarcasm.

The other cadets and officers applauded. Jordan acknowledged Captain Kanapka by smiling at him.

"Speech!" One of the cadets shouted.

Hollis hesitated as though having to work at making the decision. He surveyed the room. "I've done it," he said proudly. "But I can't fight Hitler alone."

Jordan noticed that Hollis was staring at him.

"The rest of you have to do the same!"

Some of the other cadets expressed agreement verbally and through clapping.

Jordan quelled the irritation rising in response to Hollis Boyd's arrogance. He watched Hollis receive congratulations from cadets and officers. Even Adams gave the appearance of being happy for him. Hollis whispered something to him.

"Quiet! Quiet everybody!" Adams said.

After the din died down, Hollis stepped to the front. "Just wanted to make sure I gave some credit to the good Lord," he said. "Can't forget Him!"

A smattering of hand claps and at least one "Amen" followed. Everyone then returned to their conversations as they headed for the chow hall.

Jordan saw Willie bouncing in his direction.

Willie said in a rather unpleasant tone, "I hope you know your stomachache cost me a month's pay!"

Jordan tried to hold in his laughter. "Jitterbug, did I tell you to bet? I mean, really."

"No, Hotshot, but you sure in hell didn't tell me not to."

"Hey, sucker!" Claude called to Willie as he approached them. "Let me see how my dough is holding out." He pulled out his billfold and frowned while counting the number of bills. "Getting mighty low." Then he located some bills in another pocket and smiled. "Thanks for the friendly wager, Willie."

Jordan could not hold back his laughter any longer.

Colonel Saunders had every reason to feel confident about himself. He relit a cigar. After all, he had watched five classes prior to the current one complete all phases of training. The classes had been small, and there had been a significant number of cadets who had washed out at various phases of training. Buford smiled as his eyes browsed down the records of each of the classes. Just like I told them, he thought. The more applicants they send the worse off they'll be. There can't be too many cream-of-the-crop representatives in the colored race. When my prediction comes true and they have to cancel this thing, those damned Yankees will have to start paying more attention to what I have to say. He walked over to the window and peered out across Tuskegee Airfield. At the flight line, Adams was instructing a group of cadets from the current class. At the same time there was one of the AT-6 trainers lifting into the air. He held his breath until the plane had climbed high enough to clear all buildings and trees. When it did, he did not feel elated, but he noticed neither did he experience the same sense of disappointment he had experienced at the beginning of the project. He wasn't sure what was happening to him. He certainly still expected the worse.

At 4:00 p.m. , his secretary paged him. "Washington D.C., sir. Mr. Morley's on the line."

"Hello, Buford," Morley said cheerfully. "Just called to inform you that you're about to get your wish. I know that you haven't been too happy down there."

"Well, Glenn, I did have to make a few adjustments. Quite a few," he corrected himself while chuckling. "The whole set of circumstances are a little bit different. But I think I've managed. And I guess given a little more time I---"

"You won't have to worry about that, Buford."

"Well, what I'm trying to tell you is it really ain't --- isn't quite the bother I first thought it---"

"Buford we have a new assignment for you. Give you an opportunity to come back to civilization."

"Thanks, sir."

"Bastard!" He spat out after hanging up. This was not what he wanted after all. Not now. He wanted to stay to see the total destruction of this experiment. He did not want to return

100

to Washington to be a desk jockey among a bunch of Northern know-it-alls.

That night, Buford sat in his chair. He had been sitting there at least three hours, perhaps longer. Why was he being replaced now? Being relieved of an assignment prior to completion was a new experience for him. Hard Rock Adams entered and stood at attention.

"You wanted to see me, sir?"

"That's right, Captain. I know you're wondering why, considering the hour. You needn't worry about it being an emergency. Not unless. . ." He was finding it most difficult to handle his emotions, to express what was going on inside of him. "Well, Captain, I've been ordered back to Washington."

After a pause, Adams said, "That's where you preferred to be. Right, sir?"

Saunders slumped deeper into his chair. "Not like this. Relieved after so short a time. They want me to believe this is a promotion." His laughter was hollow.

"Then it isn't, sir?"

Saunders shook his head slowly. He reached for another cigar, arose and crossed over to the window. "I don't give a damn what those smartass Northern politicians say!" He looked at Adams. "Hard Rock, not one of these 'Nigras' will ever hold a candle to you!"

"Thank you, sir, but that was a long time ago."

"Hells bells, you can still fly rings around any one of them!"

"Boyd flew his solo."

"I know. What happened to Wingate?"

"He got sick, sir. Something about a stomachache."

"I see."

"Sir, what happens to me now?"

Saunders thought about his answer. "You can be a lot

more effective in your present position."

"So, Kanapka is our new commander," Adams said wryly.

Saunders nodded. "I tried. You could have done the job, but…" He threw up his hands in a gesture of helplessness.

Adams' tone was bitter. "The story of my career."

"As long as we own the key to the kingdom, they can't get in," Saunders said. "Do you understand?"

"Yes, sir."

"You sure?"

"Yes, sir. I do."

"Good. Your job is to make sure that they don't get the key. The way I see it, I don't think we have to do much more. I think this experiment will self-destruct."

"Yes, sir." Adams' response lacked enthusiasm.

Long after Adams left, Saunders wrestled with the reasons he was reluctant to leave this command. He was not sure whether he wanted to stay and watch the 99th fail. When it did fail, he could say, "I told you so." Or could he? His whole career as commander had been filled with successes. The other alternative was to stay and add the 99th to that record. To watch them reach the point where they could attain the unthinkable, facing the enemy as fighter pilots. But the odds against that happening were so great. *So great. What the hell,* he thought. Now I don't have a choice. *Time to quit procrastinating and break the news to Ethel and Minnie.*

CHAPTER NINE

The night prior to Jordan's first solo he strolled with Terri to her apartment. It was a sultry night, and rain showers had been prevalent most of the day. The forecast was for more of the same for the next two days.

Terri said, "Are you ready?"

"As I'll ever be." As though to make up for being so preoccupied, he pulled her close and kissed her on the cheek. "But I've got a feeling that after I solo, all hell's gonna break loose!" His laughter was brief as he thought about what this could mean.

"Hard Rock's still trying to stop the program?"

"I'm convinced that he's never wanted it to succeed. The same is true for Colonel Saunders."

They walked in silence until they arrived at her apartment. Jordan embraced her.

"You know you can always leave. Quit, like some of the others." She did not sound like she meant what she was saying. "After all," she continued, "everybody here knows that you can fly. No need to prove it anymore."

He laughed. "Honey, they ain't seen nothing yet."

"All right, Jordan 'Hotshot' Wingate. Go out there and fly like you invented the word and the plane."

"And then what?"

"And then, just like you said, all hell is gonna break loose!"

They ended the date with a real good laugh.

The following morning was overcast, but the rain had stopped falling. When Jordan arrived at the plane, none other than Oscar Tate greeted him. "Man, you don't waste much time!"

Oscar's big face lit up. "Hey, I just wanted to make sure

the future ace pilot is taken care of by the best mechanic!"

"Is this bird ready?" Jordan climbed into the cockpit and squirmed around until he felt comfortable.

"Tight fit?"

"Always in these little suckers."

Oscar grinned. "Maybe you better lay off the pork chops."

"If I could just beat you to the meat server I might get to eat one pork chop every so often."

Oscar laughed. "Do you think you can top Cadet Hollis Boyd?"

"Well, I'll try." Jordan fastened himself in snugly.

Oscar said, "So to get this little crate to move, first you have to give it some throttle?"

"That's right. The engine needs some fuel."

"Needs a little drink."

"Uh huh. A big one. I see the tank's full."

"Everything's right. I told you I aim to take care of the main man."

Jordan gave him the thumbs-up sign. "Did you make all the checks? What is it, a zillion and one?"

"Just thirty-five, Hotshot. Just thirty-five."

"Okay, I do believe I'm ready to take this baby up!"

As he began his taxi down the runway, Jordan noticed Oscar scribbling something on a piece of paper. He glanced over at the group of officers and cadets gathered to watch him take off. Hard Rock was standing alone, feet spread, hands on his hips, and his expression stern. Jordan smiled at him and continued his taxi. When he neared the takeoff position, he stopped and made his final engine checks and lined up with the runway.

He raced the AT-6 down the runway, lifting it into the air as level as was possible. As he flew higher, he thought, *No tricks, just good old safe flying. Don't need to give Hard Rock any excuse to make life any harder for me.* He flew beneath most of the clouds at a conservative speed, banking the plane conservatively on the turns. "Take that, Hard Rock!" he shouted into the air. Later, his descent and landing were as conservative and flawless as were the ascent and flight. He responded to the smattering of applause from the cadets, especially from Willie, who gave him the thumbs-up sign. He also saw Terri and Sue, who now showed no visible signs of her encounter with the Montgomery policeman.

The next day Lloyd Kanapka sat at his desk thinking about Cadet Wingate's flying display. Now two cadets in this class had completed the training. Much had happened to the captain during the week. The second of the two best cadets in this class soloed, and he received orders that promoted him to the rank of major. He wanted to believe that the promotion was based totally on the results of his ability, that it was one hundred percent merited. But he could not rid himself of the certainty that the influence of his father, Major Frank Kanapka, hero of World War I, was still strong years after his death.

When Hollis Boyd arrived, Kanapka noticed his discomfort, which was much more so than Jordan's. That Boyd was a sharp military man was something all the officers knew and had admitted to one another a long time ago. "Have a seat, Cadet... How do you read your class?"

"Well, sir, I think the morale is much better now."

"I agree. Would you say that Cadet Wingate has a tremendous effect on the others?"

Hollis nodded. "That and your attitude toward us, sir."

Kanapka held up the latest copy of the Pittsburgh Courier, one of the first black newspapers in America. "Lately, I've been familiarizing myself with the *Courier* and the *Chicago Defender*," he said. "My purpose for calling you here was to assure you that along with making sure the Tuskegee Airmen get the proper training, I'm also aware that the social conditions can be better."

"Thank you, sir."

"All right, that's all."

They exchanged salutes.

"One more thing," Kanapka added. "I can't promise that every officer here shares that awareness."

"I know, sir." Hollis, now much more relaxed, smiled slightly, saluted Kanapka once more, and left. At this moment, more than at any other time since what the skeptics called an experiment began, Kanapka felt very positive. One day Wingate, Boyd, and others would get their chance to fight. He knew that's what they wanted more than anything.

Hard Rock Adams wanted to prevent Jordan Wingate from feeling that he had arrived, that there was nothing else for him to learn. Adams finished his early morning shave. Very early. Over the years in the military, he developed the habit of rising earlier than those around him. There was something about the quietness of the atmosphere he appreciated. His mouth had a stale taste, the result of smoking a pack and a half of Lucky Strikes, his daily consumption these days.

His body felt a tiredness that he began to notice more and more when he reached his fortieth birthday, and even more so when he reach his forty-first. He thought that after four months of this assignment what he needed was a leave. Even a week would do. The cigarette he lit prior to lathering his face was now little more than an ash, which fell to the cement floor.

106

His face stung from the after-shave lotion he slapped on. He lit another Lucky Strike. It was almost time to rouse the other officers out of bed. Of course, Cadet Wingate really was a hell of a pilot. He was also one of most arrogant bastards he'd ever met. So to even hint to Wingate what he really thought about him could be one of the biggest mistakes he had ever made.

Later at the flight line, Jordan watched and waited impatiently for Hard Rock Adams to finish his bantam rooster like strutting. He knew that Willie, Claude, and the others felt like he did. They simply wanted to get on with what they knew was inevitable, that one day soon they would become fighter pilots.

"Listen up!" Adams said. "We don't want you few asses who've managed to solo to get the idea you're something special." He glanced at Jordan. "Flying alone is all right if you're performing a damned air circus!"

Terri and two other nurses strolled toward them.

Adams continued, "Your survival during wartime depends on whether you can fly in formation." He glanced at Jordan again. "But why in hell am I talking about formation flying with you losers?" Looking at Jordan he continued, "Cadet, you just might succeed in flying formation!"

Terri and the other nurses passed by on the other side of the street.

"The rest of you? Hell, those nurses could probably fly rings around you right now!"

Jordan appreciated the opportunity to fly alone with

107

no instructor to accompany him. It was the primary reward for soloing. As he flew the AT-6 over the vast Alabama countryside, he had time to reflect on the beginning, the first instructions from Velma Greer and the extent of her surprise when he announced after the second lesson that he was ready to fly alone.

She and others had not believed that was his first time flying solo or escorted. He thought about the first time he heard that the Department of War was considering admitting Negroes into the Army Air Corps. Velma Greer, unlike the majority of people with whom he talked, did not attempt to discourage him of his dreams. Though he had never told her as much, her attitude had meant a great deal to him. It sustained him when self-doubts started to creep into his mind.

Now he was flying over a field full of people moving steadily in one direction. Some of them moved a little faster than others. When he descended and leveled off closer to the field, he could see that the people were black and that they were picking cotton and stuffing it into huge white cloth sacks that they were dragging behind them. He reduced his speed and his altitude to such an extent that the pickers looked up and waved. He realized that they had no way of knowing what color he was. He noticed, to his disappointment, that he did not have enough fuel to turn around and fly low without his headgear so that they could see that he was just like them. But he was sure that he would come this way again.

Back at the post game room, he located Claude and Willie shooting pool.

"Gents, you know I thought we'd been freed from slavery a long time ago."

"Well, we were according to the history books I've

read," said Claude.

Willie chalked his cue. "Any of them you haven't read, Book Man?"

"Well friend, since you can't read, I read your share."

"That's kind of you, 'fessor, mighty kind," Jordan said. "What I want to know is if we've been freed, why did I just fly over a field full of folks my complexion picking cotton?"

"I take it flying over cotton fields is a privilege earned by soloing?" said Claude.

"Now you're cooking, Book Man. Jordan earned that right."

"And if you two plan to help me and Hollis kick Hitler's butt, you'd better get yours in gear," Jordan said. He crossed over to a window and looked out at the flight line where Adams and another instructor were talking. One of the nurses strolled by. "You know, I wouldn't put it pass Hard Rock to teach some of the nurses to fly." He chuckled. "You know just to prove a point. Wouldn't it be funny if Terri and Sue, bruises and all, soloed before both of you boys?"

Willie was noticeably concerned. In a most deliberate manner he hung his scarf around his neck, put on his leather jacket and his cap and gloves.

Jordan realized that by mentioning the females as competitors he had shaken Willie more than any other method could.

"Where you going, Jitterbug?"

"To get my name on the flight schedule for tomorrow." Willie wrapped his scarf around his neck and walked swiftly toward the door. "No way on earth I'm gonna let any broad beat me flying!"

The next morning Willie proved that he was more than talk. In his usual cocky manner, he bounced toward his plane, in a short time completed his solo, and was back on the ground.

109

He winked at Sue.

As Jordan exchanged a thumbs-up sign with Willie, he wished he'd realized sooner that the thought of a woman outdoing him would push Willie's button. *Now all I have to do is locate Claude's button,* he thought.

In the early morning later that week, Jordan flew over the same cotton field he had seen previously. Flying as low as safety allowed, he noticed Negroes of various ages. Most of the males were wearing plaid shirts under faded bib overalls containing patches of various sizes. The women and young girls wore cotton print dresses and bandannas on their heads. He experienced a feeling of satisfaction and pride in response to the exuberant waving and shouting of the pickers. Not since his flights in Columbus had he felt so proud of being a Negro. Pride changed to fear as the engine coughed and sputtered and began to lose altitude. *Damn, I'm running out of fuel,* he thought. He pushed forward on the stick and headed toward the cotton field. His welcoming party scurried in all directions as he plunged toward them. He managed to clear the cotton field, touch down hard, bounce and come to a halt within a few yards of a grove of trees.

Though he realized that he was not badly injured he was not sure whether or not the plane was damaged. He needed to collect himself. The voices of the pickers grew louder as they hustled over to the airplane. When Jordan opened his eyes, he saw them surrounding the plane. Seeing him, their combined expressions became one of wide-eyed amazement.

"James, Booker, don't you all just stand there like trees!" A lusty, dark-complexioned young woman cried. "The man's in pain!" She moved and talked like she was in charge. "Ollie," she said to a squat, muscular teenager, "you and Joe can help him!"

Ollie and an older man moved to the plane.

110

Jordan, his vision nearly clear again, unbuckled his shoulder and seat straps. He dropped to the ground staggering ever so slightly, realizing that he had banged his left knee against the panel. The ones named James and Booker supported him. "Hi, kid," he called to Ollie who stared at him as though mesmerized.

The woman in charge said, "He ain't never seen one of our kind flying no airplane. I reckon none of us have."

The others agreed, smiling, staring, and touching him.

Jordan moved his legs and arms to make sure that other than the bruised knee, all that he suffered was a good jolt. "Don't think I flew too well."

James said, "I was wondering, do you always land next to cotton fields?"

Some of the others laughed robustly.

Jordan noticed that his audience now included a group of white men gathering on the road.

A young boy raced from a two-story white house splashing water from a bucket.

"Soaking your leg in some cold water ought to help," the woman assured him.

He thought about refusing the offer. But everyone else seemed to obey the woman. Why should he be different?

"Well," he said, more to her than to the others, "if I had to crash I sure am glad I picked this place, miss!"

"Doris," she responded, embarrassed, a hint of a smile exposing sparkling white teeth against her dark complexion. "Doris Caine. I could call for help."

"From where?"

She nodded toward the white house.

"You mean they'd let you use the phone?"

Ollie said, "Sister usually gets what she wants."

"Thanks." Jordan pulled his leg out of the bucket of

111

water. "But that bird just needs some gas. Then I'd better get myself back to the airfield." He tried to walk and still felt some pain.

He had heard the term "shotgun house" to describe the tiny shacks many Negroes lived in, so called because their sizes were such that bullets could travel through the front and pass through the back without impediment. Later, as he sat in a chair in what served as the kitchen and living room of the Caines, he could understand the term. The family of five, headed by Luther Caine, existed in two rooms that served the same functions as the five rooms and a bathroom of his home in Columbus. The Caines' bathroom consisted of a tin tub in which they bathed, and a primitive commode housed in a weathe-beaten shed.

"Supper's ready," said Doris. She was a tall, robust woman whose big smile was continuous. She had cooked more greens, salt pork, cornbread, and corn than the five people there could eat. But they proceeded to make a noticeable dent in the food.

"They feed you food like this at that camp?" Luther Caine said. His smile exposed a mouth full of gold fillings.

"This is the first time I've had real Southern cooking since I've been down here."

"We like to share what little bit we have," said Doris. "Make sure you get enough."

He appreciated their hospitality. At first he had been reluctant to gorge himself at the expense of Negroes living in these conditions, but had done so anyway. He finally loosened his belt.

Ollie entered and announced that his gas tank was full. For the remainder of his time there, Jordan noticed the boy's attention was fixed on his boots, jacket, but especially on his scarf.

Later, before he climbed into the plane, he exchanged a

salute with Ollie and kissed an embarrassed Doris on the cheek. The farewell the people gave him was suitable for a celebrity. As in the past, the welcome Hard Rock Adams gave him was suitable for someone who had committed a major crime.

The captain took his time with some paperwork, letting Jordan stand at attention while he shuffled stacks of memos, letters, and forms from one area of his desk to another. Then remembering that he needed to write a note or to sign his name on a piece of paper, he searched through the stack until he found it. Though he had commanded Jordan to come to his office, he completely ignored him for more than twenty minutes.

Jordan realized that Adam's aim was harassment, but he was greatly amused by his scowl each time he looked up from his paperwork, and by the way that he sat on the edge of his chair and leaned forward like a bloodthirsty boxer anxiously awaiting the bell to ring.

"I'm disappointed in you, Wind Gate," he said calmly. "Who in hell gave you permission to go whore-hopping in the cotton fields of Alabama?"

Jordan willed himself to control the anger rising within. "I didn't go whore-hopping, sir!"

Adams nearly leaped out of his seat. "Are you calling me a liar?'

"No, sir."

"That's good." He strutted back and forth. "I'm waiting for your reason for landing in the cotton field."

"My plane ran out of fuel, sir."

"Who in hell's fault was that?" The scowl increased. "Nobody counts but you, right?"

"No, sir."

"Sure, sure... I knew that sooner or later you'd do something like this. Clown!" He paced some more then returned to his desk. "After my report, if this, this mob ever becomes a squadron, it'll be without you!"

Jordan experienced a sinking feeling in the pit of his stomach. "Is that all, sir?"

"You're damned right. As of this moment flying is off limits to you!"

Jordan didn't trust himself to talk to anyone for the rest of the day. Fortunately, it was the weekend and most of the cadets had gone off the base into one of the nearby towns. In fact, the only cadet still around was Hollis Boyd. The clothing lying on his bunk was proof that he was somewhere close. Even on weekends, Hollis was too neat and orderly to leave his area looking anything but spotless. Everything that should be hung up would be. Likewise, every item was placed neatly in his footlocker, and shoes and boots were lined up under his bunk. Jordan looked in the latrine, but Hollis was not there.

Later at the post cadet club, Jordan nursed a beer. The live entertainment consisted of a pianist, bass player, and a drummer, and softly played fast-paced tunes. Two couples were jitterbugging. Hollis entered and, to Jordan's surprise, headed in his direction.

"This seat taken?"

"Not until now."

A period of awkwardness followed as Hollis surveyed the room.

"Is this your first time being in here?"

"Something like that. Yeah." Hollis hesitated and then ordered a beer. "By the way, congratulations on the solo. A bit late, but..."

"Thanks, but I'm not sure how much good it'll do now."

"I heard." He took a sip of beer and frowned. "I heard about your grounding. . . Wind Gate," he said with a smile.

"Captain Adams can't seem to fix his mouth to

pronounce it right." Jordan laughed. This was a Hollis Boyd he had not seen.

"You mean old Hard Rock."

"He's hard all right. I heard that he compared us to sparrows, yet the white pilots are compared to eagles."

Hollis nodded.

"The thing is, a sparrow has wings just like an eagle," Jordan said.

Hollis took another sip, frowned and sat the bottle down. He searched for words. "Wingate, do you realize how long I've – we've been waiting for this opportunity?"

"Sure, don't the—"

"Wait," Hollis said. "I'm a few years older than you and the others so I've been waiting a little longer."

"So?" Jordan was not quite sure where this was leading.

"You know if more of us could fly like you we'd be ready to go to war right now."

"Thanks," Jordan said.

Hollis leaned toward him and a frown replaced the smile. He spoke deliberately. "But if more of us were as unpredictable as you, we'd all be at home hating the War Department for denying us this opportunity. Wingate, I just wish you'd realize this is more than some darn football game!" He did not stay for Jordan's response.

Jordan remained seated. He chuckled at the idea of Hollis coming here, drinking. Then his humor changed to anger. Feeling a mixture of anger and anguish, he stormed out of the club.

When he arrived at the barracks, he saw Claude in front of his bunk. The erudite one checked a manual, then assumed the position of an airplane pilot.

Claude was obviously caught off guard. "Hey,

115

Hotshot."

"Look, flying a plane is simple, man! Just keep the nose down, hold the stick on turns, and don't let the instructors scare you shitless!" He rushed out of the barracks leaving Claude speechless.

Jordan was not himself the next day. He did not keep track of the time. Being an airplane pilot unable to fly was unthinkable. He watched two more classmates solo. In the barracks he kept to himself. His responses to comments from Willie and the others were little more than grunts. As much as he wanted to go to war, he could not concentrate on the business at hand. He tried to talk with Claude, but the hurt in the latter's eyes stirred disgust in him rather than sympathy. He did not so much want to offer more advice or help, but rather to strike out at him. At the rate that the cadets were soloing, it would not be too long before Claude was the only one holding up the graduation ceremonies.

Jordan could not sleep more than a couple of hours. Well before the whistle for reveille, he heard a bed squeak. Hollis was arising early to read his Bible. As he watched Hollis tiptoe toward the latrine, he controlled himself from saying anything. Feeling as he did, any word might lead to a heated verbal exchange or worse, which was something he didn't need now.

For two days he borrowed Oscar Tate's Ford and drove out over the countryside passing cotton fields and numerous dilapidated shotgun houses. He could not bring himself to stop and say hello to Doris or Ollie or any of the other people he had met there. Instead he ended each day at a bar.

At the end of the week he dropped by Terri's apartment.

Later in the car, Terri said, "Where to, Lieutenant?" She was her usual cheerful self.

116

"Anywhere, just to get away from here. I've got a bad taste in my mouth about this place." He drove in total silence a few miles. He had a taste for alcohol, a craving he had more and more in the days since his grounding by Hard Rock Adams and his run-in with Hollis.

He touched Terri's hand. He had never known a woman before with whom he felt so compatible. No, that was not quite the word. He felt comfortable, so at ease. With her he did not have to be "on." No new idea or project was necessary to impress her. He could be what he considered very dull, very ordinary. In fact, she seemed to prefer him that way as if she enjoyed his presence. He reached over and swallowed one of her hands in his, winked at her, then returned to his thoughts.

Later at the Chicken Coop, he gulped down one beer rather quickly and ordered another one. He knew that Terri wanted to protest. In fact, she opened her mouth to say something at least twice, but each time she refrained. It was too early for the band to play, even on the weekend, so it was a good excuse for him to sit. Periodically, someone he knew sauntered into the club and greeted him. A man came in with a woman clasping his arm firmly enough to assure that he did not escape. A sexy young woman, heavily made up, winked at him as she sashayed by, swinging her hips. A group of older men entered. They stayed long enough to order a drink and nurse it a while, and then they left. Jordan ordered his third beer.

"Do you plan to live here tonight, sir?" Terri's smile changed to alarm.

"We haven't danced yet, baby," he said. "Haven't heard a note of live music."

"Does it matter? By the time the band starts to play you'll be too drunk to stand up, let alone dance."

"That's what you think, ma'am." But he was still conscious enough to know that he was well beyond his limit.

117

His focus was beginning to blur. And he thought that if the music started right now and he was able to stand, he would make moves that he could never make while he was sober.

"Shine, sir?" The voice was immediately familiar.

When his vision cleared, he saw that it was Ollie, the boy from the cotton field. He sat a crudely made shoeshine box beside Jordan's chair.

"Sure. Guess I've got enough left to pay for that."

"Are you sure?" Terri whispered.

"You're the airplane driver," Ollie said. His eyes widened in recognition. "'Bout every day at the cotton field we look up to see if you're gonna land that bird again."

"Well, kid, I haven't been flying the bird lately. Long story. You wouldn't understand." He attempted to stand, but knew that he had better clear the cobwebs blurring his vision first. He propped one foot onto the shoeshine box, and he and Terri watched Ollie go to work on his shoes.

"Sure did like that scarf you was wearing 'round your neck." Ollie slacked up momentarily to inspect his handiwork.

"I know you did, kid. Like I told you, I wear it to keep my neck from chafing whenever I look for the enemy trying to sneak up on me." To Ollie's pleasure he demonstrated the technique, rotating his head to the left and to the right as far as possible each way. "I know," said Ollie, copying the technique.

"Woowee!" Jordan said. "Look at that sparkle!" The light gleamed off of the toes of each shoe.

Ollie was obviously pleased by the response. "You think you'll ever drive that bird again?"

Jordan thought about the question. He looked at Terri as though she alone had the answer. She smiled. "Yeah, kid," he said. "I, uh, think I just might." And he meant it. Somehow, someway, he would fly again. There was no way that he had come this far to be turned away. "Yeah, I'll fly again!"

Ollie gathered the can of polish and several shine rags into the box. "Sister sure would like to see you flying it again." He looked at Terri apologetically. "Me, too."

Jordan handed him a dollar bill. "Thanks, kid."

"Thanks, sir." Ollie lingered awhile, shy and unsure of his next move. He half backed out of the club, nearly running into a couple entering.

Jordan reached for Terri's hand, pulled her close and kissed her. "I've got some work to do if I'm gonna help kick Hitler's butt as a fighter pilot."

She nodded, smiled, and leaned close for another kiss.

The next evening Jordan finished shaving. On the way to his bunk he stopped and watched Claude sitting on his footlocker shining his boots. They had not said much to each other since their confrontation. Consequently, Jordan hesitated to say anything. He simply watched. They were the only two there. "You know what, Book Man?" He sat across from Claude. "Hard Rock grounded me. He didn't say I couldn't coach you."

Claude stopped shining and eyed him somewhat warily.

"Now put down that boot and listen to me." He now had Claude's full attention. "See, it all starts with confidence."

Hollis entered but did not say anything.

Claude said, "If anybody knows anything about self---confidence, it's you, Hotshot!"

"Yeah, but we're not talking about me."

"All right, my self-confidence. I've got it. See how easy it is right now!"

Jordan leaned closer. "You'll have even more confidence after you complete your solo. And I've got a plan to make sure that you do." But Claude was already starting to look doubtful. "You know what? There's an added benefit for you if you show Hard Rock you can do it. You just might cause a certain daddy to have a whole lot more pride in his son."

Claude said, "All right, Hotshot, let's hear the plan."

CHAPTER TEN

Cadet Claude McCall had to graduate. Over the months since they met, that thought had stayed constant in the back of Jordan's mind. He would solo first, and if neither Claude nor Willie had done so, he would do all that he could to help them. Now that Willie had soloed, it was Claude's turn. Jordan was convinced from early in their relationship that Claude possessed most of the attributes to be more than just an adequate pilot.

On a rather brisk windy morning, Jordan looked around and noticed the number of cadets and officers gathered to watch Claude do what many of his classmates suspected that he might not ever do. The same was true of some of the graduates of the previous classes returning to the scene of their triumphs. Claude's ineptitude had made him famous. Jordan was sure that the basis for his problems was a lack of confidence. He climbed into a plane temporarily located away from the main parking location for the squadron of planes, determined to make Claude a star.

Inside the plane, Jordan remembered Hollis Boyd's accusation, his anger, his questions about his plan for Claude. He shivered and paused awhile to collect himself. He thought of the dangers inherent in facing a former college boxing champion in condition to destroy anyone who challenged him. That, in itself, was enough for him to worry about, but there was something else. An even greater concern was what if his plan failed? What if Claude did not complete his solo even with his help? What if he froze up on the ground? What if he got off the ground and erred to the extent that he could not land safely? Worst of all, what if he crashed? How much of the blame would he have to assume? He licked his lips, dried by his anxiety. Crazy, he thought. He shook his head as if that cleared it for rational thinking. Everything would be all right. He switched the radio on as Claude taxied down the runway.

"All right, Book Man, can you hear me?"

"Loud and clear." His voice was shaking, less than assuring.

"Great! So far, so good!"

Claude said, "Wait until I do something."

"Hey, you already have!" Jordan watched him take off perfectly. "Book Man, this is gonna be one hell of a solo. Yeah, yeah, yeah! Now pull just a little more on that stick to reach a comfortable altitude!"

Claude laughed nervously, "Is there such an altitude?" He followed Jordan's direction. "Well, how am I doing Hotshot?"

"Beautiful man, simply beautiful! I think you're going to change my mind about all that reading you do!"

"Hey, I've spent as much time up here as anybody!"

Jordan said, "Calm down now. Anyway, the proof's in the way you're handling that bird. Wooweee!"

"Wingate, did anybody tell you you're a lunatic?"

"I'll accept that! Now, what's your next move?"

"I'll leave all of the fancy stuff to you. I'm just going to bank this baby, make the turn, and bring her in!"

"All right. Remember what Mother Hard Rock said about that throttle. I can hardly wait to see his face when you land!"

Claude touched down a little too quickly, bounced twice, but recovered in time to come to a stop without damaging the plane. By the reaction of the crowd, he had silenced his harshest critics once and for all.

Claude's success was cause for a celebration. Lloyd Kanapka, just recently promoted to colonel, orchestrated the pregraduation party in the post club. Jordan danced with Terri, Sue, and several of the other nurses there for the festive occasion. A six-piece band provided professional entertainment. There was enough booze that everyone who wanted to get drunk could do so, which the majority of the airmen did. Hollis was there, living proof that a person could remain sober in the midst of all of the booze flowing. Claude, a paper cup sitting precariously on his head, made his first attempt at dancing with Sue. She was having a difficult time guiding Claude while controlling her laughter. Claude sober was as stiff as a board, but Claude drunk was as flaccid as a rope.

"Cadet Wingate, let's talk a bit." It was Colonel Kanapka.

"Yes, sir." Jordan followed him, thinking that they were going to go to his office.

If so, he figured that would be a sign of trouble. He could feel the stares of the cadets as he followed Kanapka to a small room in the club.

"This will do. At ease, Wingate." Kanapka loosened his tie. "Let's make this informal." He sat on a wooden folding chair and motioned for Jordan to do the same. "I haven't heard much about your flying escapades lately." He relaxed even more. "Lieutenant Wingate, you might as well get used to being an officer."

"Thank you, sir."

"Is everything all right? The reduced flying hours?" He studied Jordan awhile. "You don't think you know all there is about combat flying?"

"No, no, sir, but Captain Adams…"

Kanapka smiled slightly. "I got his report. We both think that what you did for Cadet McCall was admirable."

"Sir?"

Kanapka rose, crossed over to the radio and touched it. "Your instructions came across loud and clear."

Jordan was surprised to know that Kanapka had been

123

listening to his instructions. "Sir."

"Listen up. Colonel Saunders and some dignitaries will arrive here from Washington, D.C., for graduation ceremonies Saturday morning. That's two days from now. I want you to lead the squadron in the flying exhibition. Is that understood?"

"Yes, sir!" Jordan could hardly control his excitement. He had been looking forward to the chance to fly again ever since Hard Rock grounded him.

After letting Jordan get a full idea of what he was saying, Kanapka continued, "Wingate, you can consider what I've shared with you as an order rather than a request. As leader of this outfit, I'm telling you what I want you to do. And if there's one thing you should know about me, it is that I don't order a cadet to do anything beyond his capabilities. Considering the people that will be here, you must know how important it is that the 99th look good. No, that's not a strong enough adjective. Your performance must be extraordinary. It must so impress the viewers that they will have no doubts, whatsoever, as to your abilities to become fighter pilots on the same level or even better than any white fighter pilot. Is that understood?"

"Totally, sir."

"Good. We both know Colonel Saunders . . . Enough said."

Outside, Jordan breathed deeply and exhaled, feeling the lifting of a great weight that he had been laboring under for a week. There was nothing the colonel could have said more important to him at this time.

The next day he wasted no time contacting Sergeant Oscar Tate. Oscar was doing some mechanical work on one of the planes. He frowned good-naturedly when he saw Jordan coming. "Hotshot, I thought your orders were not to get near a plane."

"That might have been what they were, but those orders

have been superseded."

"Superseded, huh? Since when? And by who?"

"Yesterday, by the top man."

"Kanapka. How come I haven't received a copy of those orders, sir? Almost forgot."

Jordan touched him. "You will get the orders. Trust me."

Oscar pretended to be trying to decide whether to believe him. Then he broke into his big, body shaking laughter. "Sure had you going, didn't I, Hotshot?"

"Hell, no. I'm just surprised you could keep a straight face for more than a minute."

"Liar. All right, so you're gonna lead the squadron in a formation flying exhibition tomorrow morning."

"That's right. If they'll follow me after my last stunt."

"Even Jitterbug and Book Man?"

"Especially them. I wasn't too surprised by the cold shoulder I got from Hollis and some of the others. But those two."

Oscar produced a grimy rag and wiped his face, replacing the sweat with grease. "Hotshot, I think that old problem called jealousy just might've gotten the best of our friends."

Jordan followed the chubby mechanic out of the hangar to the flight line where a large party of cadets was waiting.

"All right, Jordan Wingate, let's see if you've forgotten anything during your, ah, vacation," Claude said.

Jordan had to collect himself, so moved was he by the turnout.

"Hey, Book Man," Oscar said, "Jordan would have to quit flying for years to forget more than you know about flying." This remark brought howls from the others. "All right, Mr. Leader, you gonna fly this thing or not?"

Jordan touched Oscar. "You're darn right I am."

"Hotshot's back!" Willie pumped his hand. "Hey, Mr. Hitler, you and your Luftwaffe better look out for the Tuskegee Spookwaffe!"

"Spookwaffe! Spookwaffe!" The other cadets chanted as they cleared the way for Jordan to climb into the plane, taxi down the runway and take off as smoothly as though he had been flying every day. The cadets were still celebrating when he returned.

Hollis met him when he climbed down from the plane. "Good show, Wingate." He offered his hand. "Guess you're ready to lead us in the big show."

Jordan felt Boyd's genuineness in the firm grip of his hand, in his tone of voice, and in the warmth of his smile. "You bet."

"Good. I can hardly wait to show the good colonel how wrong he was about us. I'm sure Hard Rock already knows."

They were in the barracks. Jordan knew the importance of the next morning would prevent him from sleeping. From the moment Kanapka lifted his grounding, his energy had increased to a level that was high even for him. He hoped that at some time very soon he would feel exhausted enough to sleep, but his mind soared into outer space with reflections on his days as a football player and on his relationship with his family. There was his mother's continuous faith in him versus his sister's wavering faith. The skepticism of his father was nearly as strong as that of other people he knew. And there were many whose doubts of the black man's ability to fly, especially to fly in combat, were expressed by the news media. Years ago he promised his family he would one day become a fighter pilot. His father had said that the only way he would succeed would be to follow the example of Eugene Jacques Bullard, who in 1914 joined the French Foreign Legion and became a pilot with

126

the famous Lafayette Flying Corps. But now he would prove all of the doubters wrong. He made sure that his flight uniform was ready for tomorrow.

At midnight the lights were out, but the other cadets were as wide-awake as he was.

"Your father coming tomorrow, Claude?" Jordan said. "Coming to see his big boy soar like a bird?"

"I sure hope so. He's always busy. But he knows I'm graduating."

"He'll be here."

"Is that a guarantee?"

"Hell, yeah," Willie said. "Trust Hotshot's promises. Your old man wouldn't dare miss you doing something besides reading."

That got much agreement from the others.

"I can't wait to meet a genuine Negro politician," Jordan said. "What about yours, Hollis?"

"Definitely," Hollis responded. "Probably bring a band to celebrate. But if we don't get some sleep I don't know whether they'll have reason to do so."

Jordan and the others agreed. No more words were spoken, but the tossing and turning continued well into the early morning hours.

The weather for the graduation ceremonies could not have been more perfect unless someone had access to some special control to make it so. Jordan smiled as he thought about his mother and her prayers. 'Thanks," he whispered as he fastened himself into his seat. All of the control needles registered in the green. He felt surprisingly calm, more so than before yesterday's flight. *Why not? Yesterday was to prove to a few friends that I hadn't lost it. Now it's time to show off for a few hundred people, of which two, three at the most, might be family.* The others were total strangers. This was the time for performing. He located a stick of chewing gum.

"You 'bout ready, Hotshot?" It was Oscar Tate, his moon face creased with the ever-present smile. "Didn't come this far to quit, did you?"

"And let down that audience? You've got to be kidding!" an airman responded.

"All right then!" Jordan shouted over the radio. "It's time to show what a Tuskegee Airman is made of!" As he taxied out, he felt the rush of exuberance he had felt during his first flight in Columbus. Velma Greer's Flight School happened how long ago? Weeks? Months? Years? The bleachers, full of dignitaries and other visitors, also reminded him of Columbus. Clouds were gathering. But they were too high to prevent them taking off one by one.

"Remember what Hard Rock said about the importance of being able to fly in formation," Jordan reminded them. "Let's show him we can do it!"

"We're ready, Hotshot," Willie called. "All you have to do is lead the way!"

"That's right, Jordan! We've got a crowd of big wheels down there, some just waiting for us to screw up this whole thing!" Hollis said. "Then they can say we told you so!"

"Are we gonna give them reason to say that?"

"Hell no, Payne! That is you, isn't it, Larry?" Jordan said.

"That's a roger."

"What about you, McCall? You all right?"

"Couldn't be better. I got rid of my jitters just after takeoff!"

"Book Man, your daddy's gonna be real proud of you! Alright boys, looks like the formation couldn't be much tighter. Let's razzle-dazzle like nobody else can!"

Jordan led them in a pass-over low enough that they

could almost see the eyes of the spectators. He followed that with other maneuvers, including a picture perfect chandelle. "You men are so good I would swear you've been flying for years. I think we've dazzled them enough. Let's ground these birds!"

Later the combination of relatives, friends, and a contingent of dignitaries from Washington D.C., led by Mrs. Eleanor Roosevelt, attended the graduation. Several members of the Department of War sat on a podium along with Colonel Buford Saunders. Regardless as to what any of their initial thoughts were about the chances of this ceremony ever taking place, they each spoke in positive terms. That these vibrant, intelligent Americans would succeed was the gist of each of their messages.

"We certainly want to hear from Mrs. Roosevelt," Colonel Kanapka announced to an audience growing restless from all of the speeches they had sat through. "But before she speaks, I think you will agree that we should hear some words from the previous commander of the Tuskegee Airmen. I'm speaking of none other than Colonel Buford Saunders!"

"Uh oh," Willie murmured as he nudged Jordan. "Who knows what to expect from the good colonel?"

Jordan knew that every cadet who served under Saunders had the same concerns.

Saunders moved ponderously across the rostrum to the microphone. His face screwed up in his customary frown, he scanned the audience until his gaze settled momentarily on the cadets, then to the total audience again. "Ladies and gentlemen, this is indeed a landmark day in the history of the United States Armed Forces."

There was murmuring in the audience, as well as audible affirmative responses.

"In the beginning, many months ago, there might have

129

been a few who truly believed that they would see this day. A few, I say. There were a whole lot more who never expected to see it. I dare say many Americans never expected this program, 'experiment' as it's been called, to last more than a month, two at the most." He paused and sought the correct words. "But in our skepticism we forgot about the stuff of which human beings are made. I might add, all human beings. We forgot about pride and courage. We forgot about mental and physical toughness."

He was stationary rather than strolling back and forth as he usually did. "We forgot about the inner drive that enables us to overcome the greatest obstacles." He scanned the faces of the airmen. "I guess I have to salute this fine bunch of men and their current leader." He fixed his attention on Colonel Kanapka. "I'll close by saying that I'm proud of the role I played in bringing the program as far as I did."

Saunders' speech received the most enthusiastic response of a seemingly unending number of speeches. The loudest applause came from the airmen who knew just how hard it must have been for Saunders to even hint that he had been wrong.

Following the graduation ceremonies, which included each of the cadets being promoted to the rank of second lieutenant, the spectators joined the airmen for a combination of food and drink befitting men who had been engaged in a long, hard battle and had emerged victorious.

Jordan's sister and father greeted him. "Your mama couldn't stand the long drive," Mose said. "You know if she could've come, nothing would've kept her away."

"Well, I'll just have to come see her before we go to war."

"You never know. She could be feeling better than me by that time."

"She'd better hurry up," Jordan said. "If she waits too

long, I'll be overseas and back. Probably an ace pilot by then."

His father's eyes glistened as he looked at him. "Proud of you, boy."

"Thanks, Daddy."

"The same here," Annie added. "You sure fooled us this time. Daddy spent the first three months watching the front door, expecting you to show up any minute grinning that silly grin of yours with your bags dragging the ground."

"Will you cut that mess out?" The old man tried to keep a straight face. "I quit watching the door after the first two and a half months!" He could not contain his laughter any longer. "Now, confess how long you watched the front door and the back door, too!"

They all had a long, hard laugh.

Jordan wished that his mother was with them, but he had to admit having two skeptics here was most important. His mother would have been proud, and she would have worn her "I-knew-it-all-the-time" expression. But seeing the pride in his father's eyes as he introduced him to friends made his day. It was a time he had looked forward to since he left Columbus. Colonel Kanapka made a special effort to shake their hands. Jordan knew that was an important gesture for his father. The capper of the day was meeting Assemblyman Ed McCall and seeing the joy expressed by Claude "Book Man" McCall.

They were not about to end the celebration soon, not after what they had overcome to reach this point. They continued well after their guests departed for destinations as far away as Northern California.

CHAPTER ELEVEN

Jordan and Terri could not control their laughter at Sue's attempts to teach Claude how to dance. Book Man's awkward, zombie-like movements negated the elasticity that characterized her moves. To say that he possessed two left feet might have been an overused cliché, but it was true. It was also a gross understatement. Their exhibition compared very much with a female gyrating around a tree stump.

Later as they returned to the table, Sue said, "I think I'm going to need to freshen up after all of that activity."

"Especially by Claude," Jordan responded. "I'm surprised you could keep up with him."

"Barely, Jordan boy, barely." She burst into laughter.

Claude feigned being hurt. "Just for that, the next time I won't be so easy on you. I'll have to take your breath away with my dazzling footwork."

"Oh, please do, please do!" Sue pleaded.

When the two nurses had gone to the restroom, Jordan said, " I forgot to mention how she might react to you graduating, but you two seem to be hitting it off."

"If I can just survive the dance floor." Claude wiped sweat from his brow. "Then I suspect we'll have the opportunity to engage in something a bit more intimate than reading together."

"Why, you sly devil, you!" Jordan gave him the thumbs-up sign.

Hollis Boyd entered the club, nearly jogged to the bandleader, and whispered something in his ear. The music stopped.

"All right, men," Hollis shouted into the microphone. "We've just been alerted to pack up and move out of here. We're going overseas!"

The airmen cheered as enthusiastically as they did every time they heard that Joe Louis knocked out another heavyweight contender. They stampeded out of the club. Jordan and Claude were so excited they did not wait for Terri and Sue to return.

Finally, the Department of War had decided to send them into battle. This was what they had been waiting for, the moment of truth, and the opportunity to make Hitler eat his words. The sound of footsteps filled the sidewalks as the members of the 99th raced to their barracks. Nobody ran any harder than Jordan. When he and Claude arrived, Willie was already packing.

"Hey," he said, "did you boys decide to stay here? By the time you slowpokes get packed the war will be over."

Unfortunately, this was not the last time he would make that same declaration. During the following three months, time after time the word came to them from Colonel Kanapka that he had received orders for them to move out. Each time they would be on an emotional high. Each time adrenaline would race and excitement rise. Finally, this time they were really going. They hurriedly packed all their belongings or all that their bags would hold, and loaded them into the trucks. They scurried to one of the two public phones on the post and lined up by the hundreds to make last minute phone calls. Then they loaded into trucks to begin the first leg of the trip that would take them into the field of battle many miles from home, but each time their convoy to the train aborted when they reached the front gate.

A late afternoon in February was their latest of six false alarms. Jordan followed by the airmen, stormed into the barracks. "Damn War Department ought to decide whether we're really going anywhere or whether they're just playing games to keep our minds off suspecting that we're never going anywhere!"

Hollis said, "Don't worry, our time's coming."

133

Claude looked at Hollis incredulously. "How many times have I heard that one?"

"Look," Hollis responded, "let's think of the alerts and delays as preparation for alerts we'll have when we get overseas. I've heard there'll be plenty of them."

"Don't you mean if we go overseas? Hollis, your optimism is admirable, but . . . ."

"Have a little more patience, men. I know our time is coming! I just know it!" In the midst of absolute silence, he turned to leave. But he broke into laughter.

The others were caught off guard. They reacted in stunned silence before joining him. The laughter felt good.

"So, what do we do next?" Hollis asked. "My father taught me early in my life that patience is a virtue. Though he's not a preacher, he preached patience."

Silence reigned again as the airmen pondered their futures.

Jordan broke the silence. "To hell with patience!" The frustration he was feeling changed to anger. "Look, we've been good little boys for a long time and where has it gotten us? Where?"

"Here at Tuskegee for nearly a year!" Willie responded. "Some of the guys longer than that!"

"And you know what?" Claude said, "White boys go to combat in half that time!"

"That's right. Now listen to me, men of color," Jordan looked around as if expecting eavesdroppers. "I say let's put a little pressure on the Department of War."

"How?" asked Willie. "Without endangering the whole program?"

"No danger of that. They've put too much time and money into this thing!"

They all agreed.

134

"Okay, now we're gonna make the big wheels so mad they won't wait to ship us out of here!" Apparently mad was not the right word to use. The men needed to mull this one over. "Look, have I steered you wrong before? Any of you?"

Willie said, "No, because nobody listened to you before!"

Laughter.

"Claude."

Claude looked at him like he was the last person he should ask. "No, you haven't, Hotshot."

"All right, lead the way," Hollis said.

"Remember how your mommies and daddies used to complain about how much of a nuisance you were? How they used to say, 'Boy you sure are getting on my nerves'?"

Of course, every airman could recall such incidents.

"Well, that's what we're going to do to the white folks here."

Hollis said, "If we start here, there's no telling how far our reputations will go." His expression changed from a frown to a smile. "So what?"

The decision was not unanimous. Willie was not convinced that doing anything to upset white folks would be beneficial to their cause. And there were others who were not ready to commit. But Jordan and Hollis were convincing enough to overcome all objections.

They wasted little time. The next afternoon Jordan, Hollis, Claude, and three others strolled deliberately toward their planes.

"Hey, I've stuck with you crazy ass guys up to now," Willie called as he jogged to catch up to them. "No need to change now!"

They spent a few hours then, and a few the next two days buzzing gardens, cotton fields, and buildings of the farms

135

in the Alabama countryside, which meant they flew low enough to rattle the farm hands, the chickens, cows, pigs, and horses. And the following day as they buzzed the same farms, they had to speed up lest they become the recipients of buckshot a couple of elderly men fired at them.

Colonel Kanapka expected to hear from Colonel Saunders by 10:00 Monday morning. Almost all of his past calls had been within a minute or two of the hour. Ten forty-five was so far beyond the time that Kanapka resigned himself to the fact that he would have to initiate the call. He rearranged the pictures of his family several times, shuffled the papers on his desk even more. He checked his watch and the clock on the wall to see if the time was synchronized. He repeatedly asked his secretary whether Saunders had called. Finally, he decided he would call the colonel as soon as he returned from lunch. Buford called at 11:58.

"'Lo, Kanapka. You weren't busy were you?" Saunders drawled. "Just thought I'd call to say congratulations on the job you've done there."

"Thanks, Buford." He had never realized how gratifying it would be to talk to Saunders as an equal.

"Tell me, how in hell've you managed to handle that bunch?"

If Kanapka thought that Buford Saunders had changed his opinion about Negroes, he was wrong. "Treating them like human beings is a good start."

"Oh." Saunders sounded like he expected something more. "Well, you even convinced the wheels up here that your boys are ready for combat. Are you sure?"

"I have to give credit to the instructors, both the military and civilian ones. And of course to the airmen themselves."

"Of course." Buford had expected Kanapka to pontificate, which was the main reason he took his time

136

contacting him. The other reason was his own reaction to the speech he made at the graduation proceedings over a month ago. Rather than planning that speech, it just spewed out of him in response to the flying demonstration the airmen treated them to. The performance had such a profound effect on him that he praised them in spite of himself. Afterward he remembered the Negroes in the cotton fields. The difference had been astonishing. "You've even held down the number of complaints the good citizens down there might make."

"Well, I've tried."

"Until now, that is." Buford smiled at the thought of Kanapka squirming, waiting for him to continue. "I'm looking at a stack of letters, return addresses Tuskegee, Alabama and towns close by. Kind of disturbing. Change that to real disturbing." He retrieved one of three letters on his desk.

Kanapka worked hard to hide the sarcasm in his voice. "From some of the good Alabama citizens?"

"That is correct. One wasn't so bad, but when you get a whole shit load full."

"I see."

"Let me ask you, you really trust a bunch who'd buzz the local farms in planes paid for by the taxpayers? You really think they're ready to defend us?"

Kanapka remembered the picture on Saunders' desk of two pretty granddaughters. In fact, the old man was probably looking at them fondly right now. "Well, the men are so keyed up I don't know what they might do next."

"I see." Saunders lit a cigar. "Well, seems to me we can't condone them deliberately bothering the good citizens."

"I know. Buford, just a thought. A significant number of white men are overseas fighting the enemy." He paused to make sure he worded this response just the right way. "Some of them, perhaps many of them, won't return."

137

"I know that, Kanapka. So what's your point?"

Kanapka smiled. "Just this. We might need to equal the numbers over there. I mean the percentages. Otherwise there just might be more of them. Negro men, I mean." Saunders' silence was much more noticeable than anything he could have said. His lack of response spoke volumes of words. "There just might be more of them left here to, uh, take care of, of our families. Of our children. If you know what I mean."

There was another pause. "Ah, I think I just might," Saunders answered. He puffed on his cigar and doused it deliberately in an ashtray full of butts. The smoke drifted over the picture of his two granddaughters. Then he saw them clearly. In his mind he saw the faces of Jordan Wingate, Hollis Boyd, and other Negro airmen at Tuskegee. "Well," he said, clearing his throat, "I'll see what I can do from this end about getting them an overseas assignment."

"Thanks loads, Buford. You'll never know how much that will mean to the airmen." Kanapka's chuckle turned to outright laughter after he hung up. He knew Buford did not have the power to make the decision to send the 99th to war, but he certainly had more than just an acquaintance with those who did.

CHAPTER TWELVE

On an early Sunday evening, Second Lieutenant Jordan D. Wingate drove Oscar Tate's rickety Ford down the main street of a sleepy town consisting of a combined county jail and courthouse and a handful of mom and pop businesses. The needle on the thermometer gauge rested on the highest number. The smell of rubber hoses soaked in boiling water was powerful. "Damn! Wake up, Willie! Claude!" Jordan shouted to his passengers.

Willie jumped up, wide-awake. "Hell of a place for this buggy to break down!"

"Not to mention the time," Claude whined. He yawned and stretched, trying to come fully awake.

They could hear the sizzling of water against metal as they scrambled out of the car now engulfed in steam.

"Check in the trunk for some rags, Willie!" Jordan said after several unsuccessful attempts to unlatch the hood.

Claude was already reaching into the trunk. "Filthy as can be, but I'm sure they'll serve the purpose." He handed Jordan some parts of clothing covered with grease and oil. "Must be Oscar Tate's car."

Townspeople, both Negroes and whites, drifted out of the few drab gray houses located just outside the main street. Jordan managed to loosen the cap on the radiator, releasing more steam. "I think it's shot!"

"Good. Just what we need," groaned Claude. "The next time Sergeant Pork Chops offers us the use of this excuse for a car, we ought to string him up."

"Don't say that too loudly." Willie punched him as he nodded toward the onlookers, some of whom had drawn closer.

"We're probably the high point of their day." Jordan

139

turned to the crowd. "Hi, hello, folks." He forced a smile, trying to hide his nervousness brought on by their increasing closeness and silence, especially by the white folks.

Fifty feet away, a much-used black-and-white county sheriff's car pulled to a stop. A tall, stoutly built sheriff and two deputies, each of whom were dwarfed by the sheriff, exited and ambled in their direction.

"All right boys, don't move." The sheriff said in a high-pitched voice that belied his bulk. Though his pistol remained in the holster, his hand rested on the handle.

"What's that, sir?" Jordan asked.

"Don't move!" The sheriff's expression was menacing. "What in hell are you boys doing here?" His eyes were fixed on their uniforms.

"Looks like we're fixing this car." Jordan spat out quicker than he intended.

"Hotshot," Willie cautioned softly.

The sheriff stared at Jordan. "You boys are under arrest!"

Willie said, "For fixing a car?"

"No, for impersonating officers of the U.S. military!" the sheriff growled. "Hey, Hank, go call the Provost Marshall."

The oldest of the deputies departed.

"Southern hospitality!" Claude murmured.

The cell the military captain pushed them into had just enough space for one prisoner. It contained a wooden cot covered by a paper-thin mattress and a threadbare quilt folded to serve as both sheet and blanket. The commode was clean but without a top. The strong smells of urine, sweat, and alcohol were nauseating. There was no toilet tissue, only some beige hand tissues.

"Can we make a call?" Jordan asked.

"Hell, no. Soldier, what you can do is shut that mouth of

yours." The captain banged the cell door shut and left.

Given the lack of space, the three of them slept in shifts. While one of them slept, or tried to sleep, the other two sat on the edge of the cot. The only other space available for sitting was the commode. Until now, Jordan thought that no environment for sleeping could be as uncomfortable as sleeping in a pup tent during basic training. He was wrong.

The next morning the sound of Colonel Kanapka's voice was sweeter than they had ever imagined. As tired as Jordan was after sleeping only an hour at the most, the colonel's voice jerked him to his feet toward the cell door. Claude was not far behind. Willie, who established in the early days of the training that he could sleep lengthily and with much fervor under any conditions, took a little longer to respond.

"Captain, these men are officers in the U. S. Army Air Corps," Kanapka said, as he appeared with the Provost Marshall and Hollis Boyd.

The captain, a short, intense-looking man with the red bulbous nose of a heavy drinker, was noticeably upset. "Sir, I got a call from the sheriff to pick them up for impersonating officers."

"They are officers, Captain!"

"Yes, sir. I guess we couldn't be sure." The captain's complexion was gradually matching the redness of his nose.

"Their uniforms, Captain. Their uniforms." Kanapka's voice had an unmistakable edge of anger. "You are familiar with second lieutenant bars?"

"I am! But these men — "

"Good. Captain, I want these officers released right now."

The captain opened his mouth to respond, then thought better of it and nodded to a deputy to unlock the cell door.

Outside Jordan said, "Three cheers for fresh air." He paused, looked toward the sky, and took several deep breaths.

Willie said, "Excuse me while I drop down right here and kiss the ground!"

"Just don't take too long," Hollis cried. "We really are going overseas this time!"

A week later Sergeant Oscar Tate checked the wheels of the AT-6 trainer. The only checks left were those done in the cockpit, something he usually double-checked with the pilot. He knew that this time the orders for the 99th to go to war were for real. This time they would not get new orders that rescinded the initial orders to go overseas before they even finished packing their bags. Or what was worse, two previous times they had hurried to the front gate, their bags totally packed, only to be told they weren't going after all.

The airfield had been a beehive of activity since the orders came down. Although Oscar had a hand in packing, he had not gotten word as to whether he was going. He did not know whether he would get the opportunity to be the mechanic that made sure Hotshot Wingate's plane was ready for flight. *There,* he thought. *Not a drop of excess grease on this baby.* He reached into his jacket pocket and pulled out the sheets of paper containing his notes scribbled throughout training.

"Poke Chops, you ain't fixin' to do what I'm thinking?" Slide Rice asked with a great amount of concern. He set his toolbox down and watched Oscar force his body into the cockpit. "Guess so. Didn't you forget something?"

"No," Oscar snapped.

"Well, what 'bout your parachute?"

"Where would I put it? There ain't enough room in here for me and no parachute."

"Man, you fixin' to kill yourself and this whole program, too."

Oscar released the brake. "If I can't fly this crate by now, I don't deserve to live."

"Boy, that ain't the plane they gonna fly when they get over there."

"I know that, Slide!" Oscar shouted. "I just want to show these folks I can fly." For him this was more than a tight fit. He inhaled and held his breath as long as possible. Should he forget the whole thing? Hell, no. The speech he had made earlier about being satisfied with whatever part one could play be damned. He had not come here to be a mechanic. "I can fly this thing!" he cried to Slide as he finished making his checks. *Good, all gauges are in the green.* He began to sweat and to breathe heavily. His mouth was unusually dry. He closed the canopy. There was just enough room for him to manipulate his arm to push the throttle forward. He completed his taxi, turned into the active runway, made his run and lifted off. *Good God, what am I doing? But it's too late to worry 'bout that now.*

So far, so good. His cramped quarters made it difficult to even wipe the sweat from his brow. But he leveled the plane off and was startled by the wispy clouds he could see out each side of the canopy. Each cloud reminded him of giant puffs of smoke. He felt good knowing that he was succeeding. What he was not sure about was the vibrating, the rattling of the cabinet. *Dumb me,* he thought as he located his notes. *Maybe I'm doing something wrong.* The vibration increased, shaking his entire body. With the help of the notes, he banked the plane into a complete left turn, reversing his direction. "Oh God!" he shouted when he noticed that there was a difference in the clouds around him and what looked like smoke streaming from somewhere in the plane. Now he began to sweat profusely while feeling a cold chill inside. He was having an increasingly hard time salivating.

On the ground, Slide Rice stiffened at the sight of the

143

smoke streaming out of the plane. He noticed that Oscar was attracting an increasingly large audience.

Oscar reached for a page of notes he dropped, but his jacket sleeve caught the latch lever on the canopy and jerked it open just enough for him to feel the blast of cold air. When he tried to close the latch, the air ripped the notes out of his hand into the smoke and the clouds. Good Lord! The plane began to lose altitude. Its vibrations shook him so that he felt sure his teeth had loosened, not to mention his insides. Nausea, combined with a throbbing in his head, overcame him. Momentarily, he accepted the inevitable. He was going to crash and die before his twenty-fourth birthday. Too early. Instinctively, he guided the plane toward the airfield, pulling the rudder in an attempt to ease the speed of the landing. Not enough. At first touchdown, he winced and closed his eyes. The plane bounced once, twice, and rolled at near breakneck speed. He opened his eyes just as the plane left the runway and sped over the grass. He heard an explosion as the left wing struck a shed, spun around, and skidded to a stop.

From his dazed existence, he could hear the whine of a siren. There were voices calling, "Get out of there! Get out of that plane!" Then there was a loud hissing sound like water being poured on red hot metal. He pulled on his safety harness. Nothing. He was stuck. "Oh Lord, I ain't ready to die this soon!" he shouted. He mustered all of his strength and bolted out of the seat ripping the safety harness away from its moorings. When he thudded to the ground, the harness hanging off him, Jordan and a host of others met him.

They stopped and observed him in wide-eyed amazement.

"Darn, Pork Chops!" Jordan's eyes were fixed on the harness hanging off of the hulking sergeant. "The Krauts don't need to worry about your flying, but in hand-to-hand combat you could wipe out a whole battalion by yourself!"

The other airmen concurred wholeheartedly.

The judge, a distinguished middle-aged colonel, did not concur with Jordan's appreciative assessment of Oscar's feat, but he hinted that he was favorably impressed with the sergeant's desire to fly, if not the results. In a hastily scheduled trial, just two days after the incident, he listened to testimonies by Colonel Kanapka and several other witnesses. There were no contestants. The small courtroom was packed with members of the 99th Fighter Squadron supportive of Oscar and anxious to get this bit of business over with so they could defend their country.

Jordan and others held their collective breaths as the judge brought the trial to a speedy end in the following manner.

"Sergeant Oscar Tate, you've been found guilty of destroying U. S. Government property. Under normal circumstances, the penalty would be stiff. Stiff indeed. I say under normal circumstances." The judge paused, adjusted the bifocals sliding down his nose. "So, realizing that Sergeant Oscar Tate is guilty, we're here to determine whether to deny him the opportunity to defend his country. This is something that he and the other members of the 99th want to do in the worst way." While scanning the room full of airmen, he took a sip of water, focused on Oscar. "The fine for Sergeant Tate is the cost of the damage done to the plane, to be deducted from his pay each month, and to continue while he is serving his country as a mechanic for the 99th Fighter Squadron during their tour of duty in Europe. Case dismissed!"

Most of the airmen and staff, including Colonel Kanapka, surged to congratulate Oscar "Pork Chops" Tate.

CHAPTER THIRTEEN

Jordan Wingate slowly worked his way through the crowd of well-wishers gathered at the train depot to see the 99th Fighter Squadron off on the first leg of their journey to confront the enemy. Many of the parents who just recently had been in Tuskegee to watch their sons graduate and receive their wings had not returned. But many people, primarily Negroes from Tuskegee and other towns nearby, came to see them off. The airmen had toiled at Tuskegee Airfield long enough to make their presence felt in an even wider area in the state of Alabama. People traveled all the way from Montgomery and beyond. Though the airmen were happy to be getting this opportunity, going to war was a more somber occasion than graduating. Jordan was not surprised that the atmosphere was not as festive. Hard Rock Adams at least attended the graduation. Jordan decided the captain had chosen not to see them off when he spotted him standing close to Kanapka and other officers, close, but characteristically alone. Jordan approached him.

The nature of the occasion did not seem to affect Adams. His somber black eyes under heavy eyebrows were as cold as they were that first day.

"Sir," Jordan said, saluting him.

"Lieutenant." He returned the salute.

There was a period of awkward silence before Jordan reached into his pocket, pulled out a small, oval shaped object wrapped in white wrapping paper and handed it to Hard Rock.

The captain took the little package. A slight nod of his head was his only response. After another awkward pause, he tore the paper off a smooth, polished rock on which the word, 'Thanks' was painted. His eyes darted from the rock back to Jordan, but his expression remained as cool as ever.

"Well, thanks, sir." Jordan saluted and turned toward

146

the train.

"Wingate."

Jordan turned, smiling in response to Captain Hard Rock Adams' correct pronunciation of his name.

"You are ready." It was just a statement.

"Sir?"

"You are ready." He returned Jordan's salute and departed quickly.

Terri joined him as he watched Hard Rock. "I'll see you again?" He kissed her.

"Maybe sooner than you think, Lieutenant. I just might volunteer to join you. Not that you boys will need any nurses when you go against Hitler and that bunch."

"Try to get away." He kissed her again.

In many respects, Anzio, Italy was a long way from Tuskegee, Alabama. In Anzio, they had no opportunity to jump into Oscar Tate's or anyone else's car to drive into a local town for entertainment. In Anzio, they did not have peace of mind to go to sleep at night and know that if they were awakened in the middle of the night it was not because they were under siege by Hitler's Luftwaffe. In Anzio, they were more concerned with staying alive than with making sure their hair was the right length, their chins clean shaven, and their uniforms sharply pressed and creased in the appropriate places. In Anzio, Jordan could gaze out over the terrain and see nothing but land devastated by the terrible weapons of war.

But the social environment in Anzio bore a strong resemblance to Tuskegee, especially when the 99th came in contact with white pilots. For too long their situation here in this cold, dreary, desolate land had been all too familiar. They spent

147

most of their time trying to become attached to another unit, a fighter group preferably. But it was no go. The commanders of the fighter groups expressed no interest in a black fighter squadron.

"They'd rather remain lily-white," Claude said at first.

Others repeated the phrase one turndown after another.

Finally their luck changed. They were assigned as an escort unit for a crack bomber squadron. But what Jordan and the others thought would bring them glory and honor brought nothing but boredom and disappointment, and more devastating than anything, ridicule, often from the pilots they were escorting.

Jordan, Willie, and Claude were walking toward their quarters following a mission just completed. Returning to the home base, Willie made a landing in which the wheels of his plane had been slightly damaged.

A group of white pilots joined them. "Say, if you boys would learn to fly those little planes you just might stop wrecking so many of them!" said a pilot with a generous number of freckles and buck teeth most prominent when he smiled.

"That's right," said another one. "Most fighter pilots lose their planes to the enemy. But not these boys."

The freckled faced one laughed. "Because they'll never get close enough for the enemy to fire at them!"

Claude moved menacingly toward the pilot. "Because we spend all of our time baby-sitting you bastards!"

Jordan and Willie restrained him.

"Hey, boy," the freckled faced one sneered, "why don't you direct some of that— that animal energy against the Krauts!" However, he and the other pilot must have sensed Jordan and Willie weren't going to be successful holding Claude back for too much longer. They beat a hasty retreat.

After dinner, Hollis called a meeting of all members of

his class. The mood, as they dragged into the operations tent, was one of discouragement.

Hollis, as upbeat as usual, said, "I called this meeting to give you, no, to give us, a pep talk."

"I think it's gonna take much more than a pep talk," Jordan said.

The others agreed.

"I know, I know. What we need is a few victories."

"Now you're talking," Claude pounded a fist into his other hand. "That's the only way we're ever going to be able to hold our heads up."

The agreement of the others was longer and louder than before.

Hollis scanned the faces of the class. "Are you telling me that none of you think escorting bombers is important?"

"Hell," Jordan responded, "the white boys don't seem to think it's important!"

"Until we chase the enemy off of their asses." Hollis seemed more surprised than the others by his own choice of word.

Jordan said, "All I know is that we're fighter pilots without any victories."

"Well, so far we've only had a couple of opportunities," Hollis said. "Can't hit what we don't see."

Jordan found himself being soothed in spite of himself.

"The challenge is for us to keep our heads up!" Hollis said like a cheerleader. "The question is, are we up to meeting the challenge?"

"Hell, yes!" Claude shouted. "We sure didn't come this far to quit!"

The others agreed. The meeting ended on that high note. Time to prepare for the next mission.

"Wingate," Hollis called as Jordan turned to leave,

"let's talk."

"All right."

"I know about the sacrifice you made."

"Which one?" Jordan was honestly confused.

"If Hard Rock had his way you'd have soloed first."

"Well, maybe he thought I had at least an eye-dropper full of coordination."

They laughed as they remembered Hard Rock's remark about their lack of coordination.

Jordan said, "I think Colonel Kanapka would have made the right decision. He would have chosen you."

Hollis shook his head. "He's the one who told me what you did."

"Hey, you don't have to do this."

"Wait. Don't stop me now," said Hollis. "Saying thanks isn't that easy for me. You know, putting aside your ego like you did sure is a strong leadership quality."

Jordan laughed softly. "Let's just say I've grown up a bit." He extended his hand.

Hollis obliged him. "Haven't we all? You think we can make the Old Man proud?"

"We can sure give it the good old college try!"

Later that day the commander of the bomber group informed Jordan and Hollis that the 99th would be moving again. This time they would be attached to a fighter group. After the meeting, they informed the other members of the 99th. They all agreed that now they knew exactly what being gypsies felt like.

Colonel Dave North, the cherubic commander of the fighter group, welcomed Jordan and Hollis into his office immediately after the 99th arrived. After a hasty salute, he motioned for them to sit. He offered them piping hot coffee that not only tasted good, but also warmed them against the raw cold weather.

"Let's not waste too much time," said the commander. "We're a proud group of fighter pilots. We expect the 99th to fit in perfectly."

Jordan contained his urge to shout and grab the colonel's hand.

"Thank you, sir," Hollis said. "I have to admit that our morale level is not too high these days."

The colonel offered them a cigarette and lit one for himself. "News travels. I've heard all the accusations." He smiled, dragging on the cigarette and blew some smoke rings into the room. "Even been called crazy for thinking that you men could keep pace with us."

"Or with any white pilots," Jordan said.

Colonel North nodded in agreement.

"Sir," said Hollis, "we've heard every derogatory remark imaginable from the day each of us decided we wanted to defend our country."

North stood up. "As far as I'm concerned, this is our opportunity to prove all the doubters wrong."

Once again Jordan was on the verge of celebrating. And he knew that despite Hollis' calm demeanor he felt the same way.

In their sleeping quarters, the airmen prepared for their first mission with the 79th Fighter Group. The tension was pervasive. No attempt to cover it could alter that fact. As a squadron, they agonized over the slanderous remarks to which they'd been subjected. As much as the remarks offended them, deep down they were disappointed with themselves. As the 99th Fighter Squadron, they had something to prove.

"Men, I think our luck is about to change," Jordan announced. "I can feel it."

Hollis said, "You took the words right out of my

mouth."

Willie felt both of their foreheads. "You boys have fevers again?"

"No," said Jordan. "This time the feeling is stronger than ever."

Claude looked up from a magazine he had been browsing through. "I sure hope so. If we don't get some victories soon, America will be justified in calling us a failure. They'll never let us forget this experiment failed just like they predicted."

The following morning just after daylight they were flying over Anzio. The sky was clear of any clouds.

"Hey, Book Man," Jordan called over his radio, "I've still got that feeling about this being our day!"

"All right, we do need a victory in the worse way, Hotshot."

Hollis said, "Shouldn't be too difficult seeing the enemy."

"Shouldn't be too difficult for them to see us either," Willie reminded them.

"Listen men," Hollis said, "we don't need to do anything crazy. Have a little patience. Right?"

Claude agreed. "This sure beats the hell out of flying with that other bunch."

"That's right, Book Man!" Jordan spotted several enemy fighters heading in their direction. Apparently Claude also spotted them. Without warning, he broke away from the formation.

"Book Man, what in hell are you doing?" Jordan shouted.

"This is our chance to get the monkey off our backs!"

Those were the last words Jordan or any of the others heard from Claude. He dove like a crazed man toward five members of the Luftwaffe, firing several bursts. As the enemy planes scattered, Claude followed one of them.

"Book Man!" Jordan shouted too late. One of the enemy fighters tailing Claude fired several bursts. Smoke, followed by flames, completely engulfed his plane and sent it plunging earthward into total disintegration.

There was silence over the airways.

"Damn, Book Man," Willie murmured. "Couldn't stand the ridicule another day. Sure hope his daddy will be satisfied."

The enemy wasn't satisfied. They were heading in the direction of the group.

Jordan said, "I'm about to make my daddy proud right now!"

"Gentlemen," a member of the 79th cried, "meet Hitler's Luftwaffe!"

"Oh yeah!" Willie shouted. "Hitler, I want you to meet America's Spookwaffe!"

"Okay 99th, let's kick some butt!" Jordan shouted. They attacked with wild abandon, blasting one after another of Hitler's finest out of the sky.

ABOUT THE AUTHOR

John W. Gibson was born and raised in Columbus, Ohio. He served six years in the military in the United States and Europe, spent four years as a management trainer with McDonnell Douglas Aircraft Company in Long Beach, California, and twelve years as co-owner of Worthington Paper Company. He is a member of Toastmasters International, and has done motivational speaking in educational, civic and government settings.

John is a multi-talented writer who has written several novels, screenplays, musicals, plays and a soap opera for radio. His musicals and plays have been performed in churches, schools and community theatres in several states. His characters emanate from his rich background and often portray the conflicts African-American's face as they attempt to reach a higher socio-economic plateau in the face of white resistance or misunderstanding. Underlying all of his character relationships is a striving to communicate across racial, religious and economic lines.

A Sparrow Has Wings and Higher Heights are fictional, historical accounts of the Tuskegee Airmen prior to and after their heroics in WWII. They are Mr. Gibson's first published novels.

John currently lives in Dallas, Texas with his wife and son.

Note from the Publisher

A Sparrow Has Wings has been selected for 6th grade readers and above for its fiction based on historic factual elements.

In order to Address the Standards for Education, a Teacher's Curriculum Guide has been printed with activities designed to meet the IRA/NCTE Standards for the English Language Arts.

This teacher's guide along with answer key can be ordered directly through Half Moon Publishers *www.halfmoonent.com* (e-mail: *janice@halfmoonent.com*) or 818-415-4982 for a cost of $12.50 which includes shipping and handling plus sales tax.

Ms. Sheila Alvanell Thomas-Johnson a 7th/8th grade FORUM instructor at Adamson Middle School in Clayton County created and compiled this information as a major teaching tool to assist in the Teacher's Plan to accompany this novel. Sheila presently serves as the chairperson of the Tuskegee Airmen, Inc., National Youth Program Committee, the Director of the Atlanta chapter of Tuskegee Airmen, Inc. S.P.A.R.C.-A.C.E Summer Youth Aviation Academy, and co-sponsors the aviation club at Adamson.

Additionally, there is a sequel to this book for our more mature readers entitled, Higher Heights (ISBN#1-4184-4324-7).

Please go to the web site: *www.halfmoonent.com* or *www.authorhouse.com* for further information.

SUPPORTIVE FACTUAL DOCUMENTS

NAACP Memorandum to the President Dated October 5, 1940
Army Navy Industry Discrimination against Negroes Revealed

White House Memo - October 8, 1940 initialed by President Franklin D. Roosevelt

Response to Whitehouse Memo - October 9, 1940

Signal Corp US Army Telegram – Civilian Aide January 17, 1941

National Airmen Association – Chicago, Illinois January 18, 1942

Memo to General Eisenhower April 2, 1942 The Colored Troop Problem

Official Tuskegee Squadron Emblems for the 99th and 332nd

Tuskegee Airmen Inc., Statute dedication *"So That Others May Know…" A Tribute to the Tuskegee Airmen.*

Tuskegee Dedication: Tuskegee Airmen Incorporated

Personal Letters from:
Tuskegee Library dated October 7, 1986
Larry Anderson dated October 24, 1990
Pearl Lawson, wife of Herman "Ace" Lawson dated March 6, 1990
Edith Roberts, wife of George "Spanky" Roberts dated March 6 & 19, 1990
John "Mr. Death" Whitehead and photo dated March 6, 1990

Lineage and Honor History of the early divisions of the Tuskegee Airmen:

99th Flying Training Squadron
100th Flying Training Squadron
301st Flying Training Squadron
302nd Flying Training Squadron
332nd Flying Training Squadron

Photographs of the first Tuskegee Airmen Graduating Classes in 1942
Photographs of the Tuskegee Airmen in flight uniforms with their planes

PRESS SERVICE OF THE NATIONAL ASSOCIATION
FOR THE
ADVANCEMENT OF COLORED PEOPLE

Sandler/Airmen
Document P/2

ARTHUR B. SPINGARN
President

MARY WHITE OVINGTON
Treasurer

69 FIFTH AVENUE, NEW YORK CITY

Telephone Algonquin 4-5551

WALTER WHITE
Secretary

ROY WILKINS
Assistant Secretary

GEORGE B. MURPHY, Jr.
Publicity Assistant

BOARD OF DIRECTORS

October 5. 1940

DETAILS OF WHITE HOUSE CONFERENCE ON
ARMY-NAVY-INDUSTRY DISCRIMINATION
AGAINST NEGROES REVEALED

Memorandum of Requests Presented to President
- - - - - - - -

New York----Details of the conference dealing with discrimination against Negroes in the armed forces of the United States
which was held at the White House on September 27th were made public
today by the N.A.A.C.P.

Present at the conference were: The President, the
Secretary of the Navy, Col. Frank Knox, the Assistant Secretary of
War, Robert P. Patterson, A. Philip Randolph, President of the
Brotherhood of Sleeping Car Porters, T. Arnold Hill, of the National
Youth Administration, and Walter White, Secretary of the National
Association for the Advancement of Colored People.

The President stated to the conferees that Negro units
would be organized in all branches of the army, combat as well as
service units.

In response to inquiries about the training of Negroes as
Commissioned Officers, the use of Negro professionals such as
doctors, dentists, pharmacists and nurses, and the use of Negroes
in the Air Corps, the President stated that plans for the use of
Negroes in these capacities had not yet been developed.

The Assistant Secretary of War, Patterson stated that the
War Department planned to call for service soon Negro reserve
officers but that the date had not yet been decided upon.

As to the Navy, Col. Knox stated that while he was
sympathetic, he felt that the problem there was almost insoluble
since men have to live together on ships. Col. Knox stated that
"Southern" and "Northern" ships are impossible.

Messrs. Randolph, Hill, and White presented a memorandum
to the President and the War and Navy representatives urging the use
of Negro reserve officers and the same opportunities for training
Negroes as given to others, the opening of opportunities for training
and service in all branches of the air service, requirements that
existing units of the army and units to be established be required to
accept officers and enlisted personnel on the basis of ability
instead of race or color, the use of qualified Negro technicians,
abolition of racial discrimination in the Navy, and the appointment
of competent Negro civilians as Assistants to the Secretary of the
War and the Navy.

Abolition of the existing discrimination not only in the
armed forces but in employment of Negroes in Army arsenals, Navy

Yards, and industrial plants who have received National Defense Contracts was also urged vigorously.

Speaking on behalf of Messrs. Randolph, Hill and himself, Walter White made the following statement: "It is gratifying that opportunity has been afforded to discuss frankly with the Commander-in-Chief and with the top representatives of the Navy and Army the flagrant discrimination Negro citizens are encountering in the combat and civilian wings of National Defense. While very little was definitely promised so far as action against these barriers is concerned, we believe definite progress was made."

The complete text of the memorandum given to President Roosevelt, Col. Knox of the Navy, and Assistant Secretary of War Patterson reads:

"The following are important phases of the integration of the Negro into military aspects of the national defense program:

"1.   The use of presently available Negro reserve officers in training recruits and other forms of active service. At the same time, a policy of training additional Negro officers in all branches of the services should be announced. Present facilities and those to be provided in the future should be made available for such training.

"2.   Immediate designation of centers where Negroes may be trained for work in all branches of the aviation corps. It is not enough to train pilots alone, but in addition navigators, bombers, gunners, radio-men, and mechanics must be trained in order to facilitate full Negro participation in the air service.

"3.   Existing units of the Army and units to be established should be required to accept and select officers and enlisted personnel without regard to race.

"4.   Specialized personnel such as Negro physicians, dentists, pharmacists and officers of chemical warfare, camouflage service and the like should be integrated into the services.

"5.   The appointment of Negroes as responsible members in the various national and local agencies engaged in the administration of the Selective Service and Training Act of 1940.

"6.   The development of effective techniques for assuring the extension of the policy of integration to positions in the Navy other than the menial services to which Negroes are now restricted.

"7.   The adoption of policies and the development of techniques to assure the participation of trained Negro women as Army and Navy nurses as well as in the Red Cross.

"One of the procedures which will facilitate the achievement of these objectives is the appointment of competent Negro civilians as assistants to the Secretary of War and the Secretary of the Navy. To be effective, such assistants should be responsible directly to those Cabinet members and should be vested with authority to require the cooperation and assistance of technical and administrative personnel of those Departments in the devising of effective and orderly procedures.

In addition, there is the equally important problem of equitable participation of Negroes in employment incident to national defense, with particular reference to army arsenals, navy yards and industries having national defense contracts."

October 9, 1940.

Dear Judge Patterson:

I am returning your memo-
randum to the President as of October
eighth. The President has penciled his
O.K. and initials on this memorandum and
thereby has given his approval to the
attached statement of policy with reference
to the negro participation in national
defense.

At the President's direction,
this War Department statement of policy
was released to the press by me this
morning.

With kindest regards,

Very sincerely,

STEPHEN EARLY
Secretary to the President

Honorable Robt. P. Patterson,
The Assistant Secretary of War,
Washington, D. C.

Enclosures.

Flee 93

October 8, 1940.

MEMORANDUM TO THE PRESIDENT.

x335

As the result of a conference in your office on
September 27, 1940, on the subject of negro participation in
national defense, the attached statement of the policy of the
War Department with regard to negroes has been prepared.
This policy has been approved informally by the Secretary of   x25-T
War and the Chief of Staff. I believe that it provides a
fair and reasonable basis for the utilization of negroes in
the Army expansion program, and if you concur it will be made
effective.

Robert P. Patterson,
The Assistant Secretary of War. x25

Enclosure:
War Dept. Policy
in regard to
Negroes.

S. C. Form No. 11

Signal Corps, United States Army

Sandler/Airmen
Document P/4

Received at

War Department Message Center,
Room 3441, Munitions Building,
Washington, D. C.

WA109 TWS PAID 3=WUX NEWYORK NY JAN 17 400P 1941

HON WILLIAMS H HASTIE=
CIVILIAN AIDE TO THE SECRETARY OF WAR=

PLEASE ADVISE IF NEWYORK TIMES REPORT IS CORRECT THAT A
SEGREGATED AIRCORPS SQUADRON IS TO BE ESTABLISHED BY THE
WAR DEPARTMENT AT TUSKEGEE INSTITUTE. IF TRUE, NATIONAL
ASSOCIATION FOR THE ADVANCEMENT OF COLORED PEOPLE VIGOROUS
PROTESTS SURRENDER OF WAR DEPARTMENT TO SEGREGATION PATTER
WALTER WHITE SECRETARY. 451P.

NEWS RELEASE: January 18, 1941
FROM: National Airmen's Association
      of America Willa B. Brown Secretary
      3435 Indiana Avenue, Chicago

By Enoc P. Waters, Jr.

CHICAGO -- A strong resolution condemning the War Department's plan
to establish an all-Negro pursuit squadron as a part of the United
States Army Air Corps was adopted by the National Airmen's Association here Friday.

At the same time, the association, made up of Negro flyers throughout the country, voted to intensify its campaign to have Negroes
integrated without regard to race into the United States Army Air
Corps which presently bars Negroes.

According to under secretary of War, Patterson, the squadron consisting of a ground crew of 400 men, 33 pilots and 27 planes, will
be set up at Tuskegee Institute in Alabama where a flying field
and other facilities will be provided.

The ground crew, according to the announcement will be trained at
Chanute field Illinois for several months before going to the
southern school. The squadron, it is understood, will be commanded
by a white officer.

Cornelius R. Coffey who in addition to being the president of the
Chicago chapter of the association is also national president, in
commenting said the action taken Friday is in line with the association's policy.-

"Our fight for entrance into the air corps has been long. We don't
intend to compromise now. Both the army and navy have stressed
tradition in arguing against the abolition of segregated units.

"In the air corps there is no tradition either favorable or unfavorable to complete racial interrgation. If we permit the establishment of a Negro unit, it will be establishing a precedent which will
be hard to break down.

"We'd rather be excluded," Coffey said, "than to be segregated.
There's no constitutional support for segregated units and the only
traditions existing in aviation as I know it are ones which would
make complete integration sane and logical."

Coffey is director of the aviation school at Harlem Airport which
handles flight training for a non-college and an advanced Civil Aeronautics Administration program, in both of which Negroes and whites
have participated without friction.

Willa B. Brown, secretary of the association, and coordinator for
Chicago's CAA programs, held up the Civilian Pilot Training Program
as an example of a successful interracial project in aviation.

"There is no segregation in the CAA programs," she said, "and there
have been no race riots or violence because of this fact. I think
the War Department is attempting to inject the racial issue where
none has existed in the past."

She described the CAA and the National defense aviation classes at
Wendell Phillips high school in Chicago where at least a third of
each group is white. All instructors are Negroes she said, and
there is no resentment on the part of the whites because of this.

"One of the first 10 youngsters to win flight scholarships under our
non-college program early last year," she said, "was a white youth,
Chester Krupa, who received his private pilot's license along with
nine Negroes, one of them a girl.

"I don't see why this same spirit of interracial cooperation cannot
be carried over into the army air corps."

As an afterthought she mentioned that one of the instructor's at
Coffey's school, the largest private school controlled by Negroes,
is white.

The National Airmen's association was organized in Chicago in February 1939 and includes in its membership practically all Negro
flyers from some of the earliest pioneers to CAA students. Most of
the Negro CAA flight and ground instructors are members. The organization does not bar white members, in fact the Chicago chapter has
had several white members.

A 43-inch trophy, the coveted award of all Negro flyers, is the
Dwight Green trophy presented the organization in 1939 by the present governor of Illinois.

WAR DEPARTMENT

WAR DEPARTMENT GENERAL STAFF

OPERATIONS DIVISION

WASHINGTON

Sandler/Airmen
Document P/7

CONFIDENTIAL

April 2, 1942

MEMORANDUM FOR GENERAL EISENHOWER:

Subject: The Colored Troop Problem.

I.   GENERAL OUTLINE OF PROBLEM.

The utilization of colored units is a problem that defies rigorous analysis because of the intangible nature of such factors as racial prejudice, social implications, combat efficiency, and international relations. War Department correspondence on this subject reveals that a sincere and whole-hearted effort has been made by the Department to utilize colored troops efficiently and in their proportion to the population ratio, and to provide opportunities and treatment equal to the white soldier. This approach to a solution has not received the appreciation of groups, or individuals, sponsoring advancement of the Negro race or of the general public.

The colored problem must be considered in the light of its effect upon the efficiency of our military effort. By relating its various phases to that consideration, many of the social factors become susceptible of popular under-standing and appreciation, and the established policies of the War Department appear logical rather than arbitrary.

II.   FACTORS OF PROBLEM.

1.   The Colored Soldier.

a.   From the standpoint of military efficiency, the lower average in-telligence rating of colored selectees (Tab A) is an obstacle to broad employment of colored soldiers throughout a modern, highly mechanized army. This limitation has been stressed by many officers who have had training supervision over colored units (Tab B) and is one which is not fully appreciated by civilians sponsoring Negro advancement. Lack of an educational background, plus the apparent lack of inherent natural mechanical adaptability, almost prohibits satisfactory training of mechanical specialists from colored units. Those who point out that Negroes can be educated and trained within the Army fail to evaluate the time factor involved. At present, the Army cannot perform the function of an educational institution for the individual and at the same time prepare a large, efficient, fighting force quickly. Training speed is essential and only those who are fitted for specialist or officer training, be they white or colored, can be permitted to utilize training facilities if efficiency is to result.

-1-

CONFIDENTIAL

b. This educational deficiency limits the type of units which should be activated from colored selectees. That these units are largely non-technical and often labor units, is not the desire of the War Department but results from the necessity to use colored troops where they can function most effectively.

c. The individual colored soldier, under the proper leadership, has proven to be satisfactory. He is tractable, adaptable to army life, a willing worker and generally has a high morale (Tab B). He reacts favorably to proper leadership, which has to be sympathetic, yet firm. He requires more rigid supervision to maintain good internal discipline and more intimate attention with regard to welfare but, in turn, he is loyal to those officers who have his confidence and trust. There is nothing to indicate that he is a troublemaker or that the frequency rate of court martial offenses is higher in colored units than it is in white units.

d. The modern Negro is more race conscious and apparently highly sensitive to real or imagined unjustices or discrimination. Where he is kept among his fellows and provided with the same living and recreational facilities as are white soldiers, no trouble may be expected. While there have been sporadic outbursts of racial disturbances, these almost without exception have occurred in smaller towns and investigation of the provocative incidents indicates that these derelictions in conduct were not all onesided affairs (Tab C). Intelligence Division reports suggest that some of these disturbances were the result of subversive efforts to foster race hatred (Tab D).

e. The colored soldier requires considerably more training to maintain the tactical efficiency of his unit. However, once he has learned a job well, he performs it satisfactorily and, apparently being less ambitious than the white soldier, is more content. The colored soldier lacks the initiative, imagination, and ingenuity required when routine breaks down. This increases the need for reliable leadership for the colored soldier.

2. The Colored Officer.

a. The colored officer presents more of a problem than the individual soldier primarily because of the inherent tradition which prevents white and colored peoples from mixing socially. Segregation of a few colored officers is more difficult than the segregation of large groups of colored enlisted men. While the problem is not acute at this time, under the War Department policy of providing equal opportunity for all qualified officer candidate material regardless of race, its need for solution may be expected to grow in direct proportion to the number of colored officers that are commissioned from Officer Candidate Schools.

b. The colored officer functions best in a professional capacity. Higher education among colored people tends toward law, medicine, teaching, and similar vocations rather than mechanical arts and sciences. Thus, the educational background suggests employment of the colored component in certain of the services rather than the combat branches. For example,

-2-

the Medical Corps (Tab B) reports the successful development of medical administrative officers and laboratory technicians from colored selectees. The Ordnance Department, on the other hand, reports difficulty in developing qualified ordnance specialists.

c. Probably the most important consideration that confronts the War Department in the employment of colored officers is that of leadership qualifications. Although, in certain instances colored officers have been excellent leaders, enlisted men function generally more efficiently under white officers. Officers experienced with colored troops lay this to the lack of confidence on the part of the colored enlisted men in the colored officer. This may be the reason why discipline and training in many all-colored units have been of a lower order than in those units with white officers. If this under-lying lack of trust and confidence in colored officers is basic with the Negro enlisted men, all-colored units cannot be expected to function efficiently no matter how long or effective the training program.

3. The Colored Tactical Unit.

a. It is believed that the colored element of our population is willing to share the battle losses which will be the price of a military success. However, the ultimate test of a military unit is its performance in combat.

b. There are conflicting reports on the performance of colored units in World War I, but there is a general consensus of opinion that colored units are inferior to the performance of white troops, except for service duties. This apparent weakness is believed to bear some relation to the degree of individual combat required. Due to the inherent psychology of the colored race and their need for leadership, it is believed that, when Negro troops are used in combat, they will function best in units where crew-operated materiel predominates.

c. If military efficiency dictates the use of white officers in colored combat units, a place must be found elsewhere for the employment of colored officers. A solution to this problem may be the use of colored officers with all-colored service units and for various appropriate administrative duties at post, camps, or stations where colored units are stationed.

d. At the present time, the greatest single difficulty experienced in efficient use of colored units is that of the employment of those units whose training has progressed to a point where they can be of tactical value. Modern defense requires numerous scattered small detachments of special service troops, for guard duty, transportation, antiaircraft protection, as well as the strategic deployment of tactical units over large areas. Attempts to place Negro troops in communities

-3-

for such purposes almost always meet with vigorous protests.

e. The use of colored troops in the present theaters of operations or overseas bases likewise meets with protests from others of the United Nations (Tab E.) Every country has apparently valid reasons for protesting contemplated movements of American colored units to its shores.

f. It is obvious that colored units, no matter how well-trained or in what great numbers, are valueless to the military effort if they cannot be employed where and when needed. More than that, the training and equipping of colored units under such circumstances is a dissipation of effort, manpower, and equipment which a nation engaged in War cannot afford. It is also obvious that a serious internal situation would develop if trained negro troops had to be held immobile in the continental U. S. while only white troops were sent to the firing line.

III. WAR DEPARTMENT POLICIES

1. The War Department has required that colored troops be given identical treatment and equal opportunities with white troops. Every effort has been made to eliminate discrimination, racial prejudice, and intentional or unintentional slighting of the colored soldier. It is the policy of the War Department to see that all American Soldiers have the same living and recreational facilities while in garrison and to share equally hardships in the field.

2. While segregation is essential to morale and harmony of both white and colored troops, segregation as practiced in the army is that of physical separation of military units and not that of inferior or superior groups. Colored soldiers are accorded the same treatment as white soldiers from the time they are inducted. White officers have been relieved for failure to carry out instructions in these respects. That the policies thus established are sound is evidenced by the lack of any serious trouble between white and colored soldiers within the confines of military stations.

3. By creating colored units in practically every branch and service (Tab F), the War Department has endeavored to remove any semblance of inferiority or discrimination with respect to ability. Two colored divisions, a pursuit squadron and a station hospital are among the numerous combat and service colored units authorized for 1942. Specialist and officer training for qualified colored selectees is provided on exactly the same basis as that for white personnel.

-4-

4. There is nothing in the War Department policy, or in the efforts to enforce that policy, to justify charges of injustice or discrimination against the colored race. Isolated cases where personal feelings of officers or white troops have resulted in racial disturbances have been dealt with promptly and effectively.

5. These policies have practically eliminated the colored problem, as such, within the Army. If they can be maintained without political or civil interference, they will achieve the objective of a balanced, efficient military force in which colored and white alike will have equal responsibilities and respect.

IV. CONCLUSIONS.

1. In general the use of colored troops is necessary to the conservation of man power, particularly so if we are to have an Army of the order of ten million men.

2. In the formation of colored units, consideration must be given to the limitations imposed by the lower average intelligence of the colored soldier and the need for excellent leadership and supervision.

3. The War Department has accepted responsibility for developing efficient colored units and has established policies under which there is no discrimination between the white and colored races. The War Department policies are believed to be sound.

4. Practically all of the troubles experienced with colored troops can be traced to one or more of the following causes:

a. The zealous activities of individuals and groups devoted to Negro welfare and advancement whose ambitions for the race as a whole often exceed the capacity of the individuals within it to fulfill the aspirations of their exponents. These elements promote discontent and an inferiority complex among the troops by magnifying imaginary injuries or by false statements. The Negro press is particularly at fault.

b. The traditional prejudice against Negroes which is an inherent trait of the white race.

c. The activities of subversive elements who find in racial prejudice a fertile field in which to foment trouble among both whites and Negroes.

5. A small percentage of colored officers may be absorbed without harm and efficiently used, providing that they are as carefully selected and as quickly reclassified as white officers, and that no arbitrary attempt is made to maintain their numbers above the natural

-5-

figure that would result from above processes. It is believed
that those Negro officers who meet the standard will take pride in
supporting the Army rather than racial fanatics.

6. The low average intelligence of the colored selectee
will call for longer periods of training. A smaller percentage of
trained troops will result from training centers of a given capacity
or from a given induction rate. This fact must be accepted in the
interests of full exploitation of man power. It must not cause a
decline in the standard to be exacted through an attempt to push
fixed quotas through a given program faster than the ability of the
troops concerned will permit.

7. Colored units should be considered as suitable for
service in any part of the country where they are needed. Where
prejudice still causes disturbances, individual local offenders
should be held fully responsible.

8. The attitude of the general public toward receiving
colored units in their communities is definitely unfavorable. However, proper preparations and education among civic groups within
the community concerning the military necessity of such employment
of troops will mitigate undesirable effects.

9. While military necessity adequately justifies our use
of colored troops, the importance of an example of racial cooperation
must not be overlooked at a time when so much hinges upon the actions
of India and China.

V. RECOMMENDATIONS.

1. That the present policies of the War Department be
continued and that action to enforce their spirit as well as their
letter be unremitting.

2. That appropriate agencies intensify their activity
to investigate, apprehend, and bring to trial all agents provocateurs
of both races whose actions are such as to incite race riots or
promote dissatisfaction among any groups of troops.

3. That discreet measures be taken to acquaint all troops
and affected communities with the military necessity for the use of
Negro troops, the attempts which will be made by the enemy to instigate
and exploit race riots, and the disasterous consequences to result
if both races fight here instead of fighting the enemy.

4. That efforts to gain acquiescence from allied govern-
ments to use colored troops abroad, continue.

 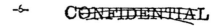

99th Flying Training Squadron

332nd Flying Training Squadron

So That Others May Know —

A Tribute To The

TUSKEGEE AIRMAN

For more information, please contact:

Joseph Blades, Lt. Col. USAF (Ret.)
3063 Whileaway Circle East
Colorado Springs, Colorado 80917

So That Others May Know—

In the rarefied air of Colorado Springs, cadets of the United States Air Force Academy compete in a serious struggle to master the elements, the curricula, and the challenge of becoming one of the elite of the world's most technical and sophisticated air forces. The emphasis, as it has always been, is duty, honor, country – and so it shall remain. Daily pervading the consciousness of these future leaders are the myriad memorabilia, rich in the history of our country from its colorful beginning to its complex present. Washington, Crockett, Bowie, Nelson, MacArthur, Eisenhower, Glenn and Slayton are but a few of the long list of names indelibly etched into the memories of doolies and graduating lieutenants. The texture of this 'long blue line' mirrors the ethnic cross-section of our nation. And yet – one would search among the many artifacts in vain, in any attempt to determine the historical introduction of members of the largest minority as full-fledged entities. On the surface it seems as though this is the way it should be – one, concentrated mixture of Americans integrated into the incredible fighting machine known so long and so well throughout the world. Such was not always the case however, and a small group of black pioneers, now waning in number, who partook in a relatively unpublicized, ill-motivated experiment to earn the right to be a part of the rich military history of our nation, cannot ignore, forget, or take lightly their role. Nor can those who carry the shield today neglect the lessons learned yesterday lest they dare risk meeting them as problems tomorrow. To this end, the Tuskegee Airmen Inc. initially composed of the remnants of the experimental group, propose to proffer a statue of a black flyer to the Air Force Academy. It would be emblematic of their sacrifices and devotion as an enduring stonemark noting the entry of the black pilot into the 'wild blue yonder' ... the beginning of the end of organized bigotry as a viable way of military life.

SOME LITTLE KNOWN FACTS

* America really did have a segregated Air Force in World War II.

* During the war, 992 Black aviators were trained at Tuskegee Institute, Alabama.

* The Tuskegee Airmen flew more than 15,000 sorties and completed over 1500 missions.

* The Tuskegee Airmen never lost an escorted bomber to enemy fighters.

* The all black 332nd Fighter Group was made up of four squadrons, the 99th, the 100th, the 301st and the 302nd.

* Black aviators destroyed 409 enemy aircraft, sank an enemy destroyer, destroyed rail traffic, coast watching surveillance stations and hundreds of vehicles on strafing missions.

* Feared and respected by the Germans, the Tuskegee Airmen were known to them as the "Schwartze Vogelmenschen" — Black Birdmen.

* The Tuskegee Airmen are an important part of Air Force history and must be remembered for their outstanding contributions to that heritage.

* For every black pilot there were ten other military or civilian black men and women in a ground support role, a virtual black Air Force.

The Hooks Jones Chapter of the Tuskegee Airmen, Inc. is involved in the exciting project of placing a statue of a Black WWII pilot on the grounds of the United States Air Force Academy. The statue along with its base will measure eight feet high. A meaningful inscription will be engraved on the base. One of the original Tuskegee Airmen and internationally known artist, Clarence L. Shivers, was commissioned by the Chapter to create this work and arrangements have been made with a foundry to produce the final bronze casting. We have been given special rates by both Shivers and the foundry. However, a substantial amount of money still must be raised to complete this project.

WON'T YOU JOIN US IN THIS EFFORT?

Please make all checks payable to:

AFA/TAI STATUE FUND

Please forward to:

AFA-TAI Statue Fund
P.O. Box 25952
Colorado Springs, CO 80936-5952

Tuskegee Airmen, Incorporated
Established 1972

THE TUSKEGEE AIRMEN

National Officers

NANCY LEFTENANT-COLON
President
OMAR B. BLAIR
First Vice-President
RADM WALTER J. DAVIS, JR.
Second Vice-President
JULIUS D. WASHINGTON
Executive Secretary
TRUMAN B. McDUFFIE
Corresponding Secretary
HENRY P. HERVEY
Treasurer
JUDGE EARL E. STRAYHORN
Parliamentarian
WILLIAM R. MILTON
Historian
JOHN D. SILVERA
Public Relations Officer

Regional Presidents

IRA J. O'NEAL, JR.
Eastern
FELIX J. KIRKPATRICK
Central
WILLIAM H. HOLLOMAN, III
Western

National Past Presidents

JOHN J. SUGGS
Washington, DC. 1972-1975
SPANN WATSON
Westbury, NY. 1973-1974
WILLIAM E. BROADWATER
Providence PA. 1975-1977
HANNIBAL M. COX, JR.
Miami, FL. 1977-1981
JEAN R. ESQUERRE
Greenlawn, NY 1981-1983
CHARLES E. McGEE
Kansas City, MO. 1983-1985
HENRY P. BOWMAN
Los Angeles, CA. 1985-1987
JOHN L. WHITEHEAD, JR.
Sacramento, CA 1987-1989

Due to the rigid pattern of racial segregation that pre-
vailed in the United States during World War II, Black
military aviators were trained at an isolated training
complex near the town of Tuskegee, Alabama, and at Tuskegee
Institute. Four hundred and fifty Black fighter pilots
under the command of Col. Benjamin O. Davis, Jr. (who was
later to become the U.S. Air Force's first Black Lt. Genera
fought in the aerial war over North Africa, Sicily and
Europe flying, in succession, P-40, P-39, P-47 and P-51
type aircraft. These gallant men flew 15,553 sorties and
completed 1578 missions with the 12th Tactical U.S. Army
Air Force and the 15th Strategic U.S. Army Air Force.

They were called the "Schwartze Vogelmenschen" (Black
Birdmen) by the Germans who both feared and respected them.
White America bomber crews reverently referred to them as
"The Black Redtail Angels" because of their reputation for
not losing bombers to enemy fighters as they provided
fighter escort to bombing missions over strategic targets
in Europe.

The 99th Fighter Squadron which had already distinguished
itself over North Africa, Sicily, and Anzio was joined
with three more Black squadrons; the 100th, the 301st,
and the 302nd to be designated as the 332nd Fighter Group.
From Italian bases they also destroyed enemy rail traffic,
coast watching surveillance stations and hundreds of vehicles
on air-to-ground strafing missions. Sixty-six of these
pilots were killed in aerial combat while another thirty-
two were shot down and captured as prisoners of war.

These Black Airmen came home with 150 Distinguished Flying
Crosses, Legions of Merit and The Red Star of Yugoslavia.

Other Black pilots, navigators, bombardiers and crewmen
who were trained for medium bombardment duty were formed
along with 332nd combat returnees into the 477th Composite
Fighter-Bomber Group (B-25s and P-47s). This group never
entered combat, because of the surrender of Germany and
Japan in 1945. Significantly, the 477th's demands for
parity and recognition as competent military professionals
combined with the magnificent wartime record of the 99th
and the 332nd led to a review of the U.S. War Department's
racial policies.

For every Black pilot there were ten other civilian or military Black
men and women on ground support duty. Many of these men and women
remained in the military service during the post-World War II era and
spearheaded the integration of the armed forces of the United States
with their integration into the U.S. Air Force in 1949. Their
success and achievement is evidenced by the elevation of three of
these pioneers to flag rank; the late General Daniel "Chappie" James,
our nation's first Black Four-Star General, Lt. General Benjamin O.
Davis, Jr., USAF, retired, and Major General Lucius Theus, USAF,
retired.

Major achievements are attributable to many of the Tuskegee Airmen
who returned to civilian life and earned positions of leadership and
respect as businessmen, corporate executives, religious leaders,
lawyers, doctors, bankers, educators and political leaders.

Nearly thirty years of anonymity were ended in 1972 with the founding
of Tuskegee Airmen, Inc. at Detroit, Michigan. Organized as a non-
military and non-profit national entity, Tuskegee Airmen, Inc.,
exists primarily to motivate and inspire young Americans to become
participants in our nation's society and its democratic process.

The Tuskegee Airmen National Scholarship Fund is the national
organization's principal program. Since 1978, the Fund has awarded
nearly $300,000 in grants to selected students who are pursuing
careers in aviation or aerospace. Other philanthropic endeavors of
the Tuskegee Airmen include the establishment of a museum at historic
Fort Wayne in Detroit, Michigan, which serves as a repository for the
memorabilia and archives of the Tuskegee Airmen; the dedication of a
monument to World War II Tuskegee Airmen at the Air Force Museum and
the dedication of a gift to the United States Air Force Academy of a
lifestyle statue of a World War II Tuskegee Airman.

With 32 chapters located in major cities throughout the United
States, Europe, and in Japan, the membership of Tuskegee Airmen,
Inc., is made up, principally, of armed forces veterans and active
duty personnel representing all of the branches of the military. It
also includes a growing number of civilians who demonstrate sincere
interest in enhancing the goals and objectives of the organization.
All officers and directors of the organization serve without salary
or fee.

Two Tuskegee Airmen, both retired USAF Colonels, share the
distinction of having flown combat missions as fighter pilots in
World War II, the Korean War, and the War in Vietnam: Hanibal Cox
(deceased), and Charles McGee. Three other Tuskegee Airmen, Lt. Col.
John "Mr. Death" Whitehead, USAF Retired Lt. Col. Bill Holloman, USAF
Retired, and Lt. Col. George Hardy, USAF Retired, flew combat in
Vietnam in other type aircraft.

For more information contact: John Silvera
                                 (213)277-2000

Washington Collection
Hollis Burke Frissell Library
Tuskegee University
Tuskegee, Alabama 36088
October 7, 1986

Mr. John Gibson
4824 Graham Court
The Colony, Texas 75056

Dear Mr. Gibson:

Enclosed with this letter you will find as much information
that I can send to you about the Tuskegee Airmen. More
information is available about them here, but cannot be
photocopied and mailed to you.

We do have the book, Tuskegee Airmen, Inc.--Tuskegee Experience,
by Tuskegee Airmen, Inc., that you can borrow through inter
library loan.

Your interest in the Tuskegee Airmen is appreciated and I hope
that you can some day plan a trip down here to see the campus
and city where they trained. It's an experience that everyone
should have.

If I can be of help to you again, please do let me know.

                              Yours truly,

                              Ms. Linda K. Harvey
                              Archivist Assistant

Enclosures

24 Oct. 1990

Dear Janice,

I am sending, John, a copy of the same material that is contained in this packet.

First, please accept my sincerest apology for taking so long to send you this message.

I have attempted to write this message many times during the past several weeks. Whenever I get involved in writing or talking about the Tuskegee Experience, I have a tendency to cover the many aspects of this historical period in too much detail.

I have read and studied the script "A Sparrow Has Wings."

The story line captures the overall realism of the Tuskegee Airmen (experiment) prior to and including World War II.

Since I lived and worked in the midst of that historic endeavor, I can relate to and recall many aspect of that milestone.

I sincerely believe your basic story line can be developed into either a dynamic Television Miniseries or a weekly television series.

Sincerely,
Larry Anderson
(Former Director Aviation Cadet Grnd. Trng. Primary

Mar 6, 1990

To Whomever It May Concern,

In 1974-75 John W. Gibson interviewed Herman "Ace" Lawson and I about his experiences as a member of the Tuskegee Airmen in World War II.

Sincerely

Pearl Lawson
Pearl Lawson

Good luck. Hope he will be able to see "a sparrow has wings" some day. So all of the Best

Ace & Pearl

Mar 6, 1990

To Whomever It May Concern,

     In 1974-75 John W. Gibson interviewed My husband George
"Spanky" Roberts and me about his experiences as a leader of
the Tuskegee Airmen (99th Fighter Squadron) during World War
II.

Sincerely *Edith Roberts*
Edith Roberts   3/19/90

3/19/90

Dear Mr. Gibson,

     It was good to hear from
you. Pearl Lawson called me
one day regarding her conversation
with you. I had wondered what
happened to you.

     I remember very well the
visit you made to our home.
Yes, there finally seems to be
much interest in the Tuskegee
Airmen — better late than never,
I suppose. I just regret that so
many of our loved ones are
not around to (hopefully) rejoice
in the final results.

     I wish you much success
in your efforts.   Sincerely,
                    Edith Roberts

Tuskegee Airmen, Incorporated

Established 1972

4217 American River Drive
Sacramento, CA 95864
March 6,1990

To Whom It May Concern:

This is to confirm that John W. Gibson did during the mid 1970's interview me and a number of other person living in the Sacramento area about our experiences with the 332nd Fighter Group while stationed in Africa and Italy during World War II. It was explained to me at that time this interview was being done in order that he might develop and write a screen script depicting the exploits of the Group and also it's accomplishments during the war.

I was a member of the 301st Fighter Squadron, 332nd Fighter Group in Italy having flown 19 combat missions with the Group.

I am now a member of The Tuskegee Air Inc., having served on the Board of Directors since 1974, as First Vice President from 1985-1987, and President from 1987-1989.

Sincerely,

John L. Whitehead, Jr.
Lt. Col. USAF (Ret.)
Immediate Past President

1st Lt. John "Mr. Death" Whitehead, of the post war 332nd FW, 100th F.S.

Lineage and Honors History
of the
99th FLYING TRAINING SQUADRON

Lineage Constituted 99th Pursuit Squadron on 19 Mar 1941. Activated on 22 Mar 1941. Redesignated: 99th Fighter Squadron on 15 May 1942; 99th Fighter Squadron, Single Engine, on 28 Feb 1944. Inactivated on 1 Jul 1949. Redesignated 99th Flying Training Squadron on 29 Apr 1988. Activated on 1 Jul 1988. Inactivated on 1 Apr 1993. Activated on 14 May 1993.

Assignments Army Air Corps, 22 Mar 1941; Air Corps Technical Training Command, 26 Mar 1941; Southeast Air Corps (later, Southeast Army Air Forces) Training Center, 5 Nov 1941 (attached to III Fighter Command, 19 Aug 1942–c. 2 Apr 1943); Twelfth Air Force, 24 Apr 1943; XII Air Support (later, XII Tactical Air) Command, 28 May 1943 (attached to 33d Fighter Group, 29 May 1943; 324th Fighter Group, c. 29 Jun 1943; 33d Fighter Group, 19 Jul 1943; 79th Fighter Group, 16 Oct 1943; 324th Fighter Group, 1 Apr–6 Jun 1944); 332d Fighter Group, 1 May 1944 (attached to 86th Fighter Group, 11–30 Jun 1944); 477th Composite Group, 22 Jun 1945; 332d Fighter Group, 1 Jul 1947–1 Jul 1949.
82d Flying Training Wing, 1 Jun 1988; 82d Operations Group, 15 Dec 1991–1 Apr 1993. 12th Operations Group, 14 May 1993–.

Stations Chanute Field, IL, 22 Mar 1941; Maxwell Field, AL, 5 Nov 1941; Tuskegee, AL, 10 Nov 1941–2 Apr 1943; Casablanca, French Morocco, 24 Apr 1943; Qued N'ja, French Morocco, 29 Apr 1943; Fardjouna, Tunisia, 7 Jun 1943; Licata, Sicily, 28 Jul 1943; Termini, Sicily, 4 Sep 1943; Barcellona, Sicily, 17 Sep 1943; Foggia, Italy, 17 Oct 1943; Madna, Italy, 22 Nov 1943; Capodichino, Italy, 16 Jan 1944; Cercola, Italy, 2 Apr 1944; Pignataro, Italy, 10 May 1944; Ciampino, Italy, 11 Jun 1944; Orbetello, Italy, 17 Jun 1944; Ramitelli, Italy, 6 Jul 1944; Cattolica, Italy, c. 5 May–Jun 1945; Godman Field, KY, 22 Jun 1945; Lockbourne AAB (later, AFB), OH, 13 Mar 1946–1 Jul 1949. Williams AFB, AZ, 1 Jun 1988–1 Apr 1993. Randolph AFB, TX, 14 May 1993–.

Aircraft P–40, 1943–1944; P–39, 1944; P–51, 1944–1945; P–47, 1944, 1945–1949. T–38, 1988–1993.

Operations Organized as the first Black flying unit in the Air Corps. Combat in MTO and ETO, 2 Jun 1943–30 Apr 1945. Undergraduate pilot training, 1988–1993.

Honors

Service Streamers. World War II American Theater.

Campaign Streamers. World War II: Sicily; Naples-Foggia; Anzio; Rome-Arno; Southern France; North Apennines; Po Valley; Air Offensive, Europe; Normandy; Northern France; Rhineland; Central Europe; Air Combat,

EAME Theater.

Armed Forces Expeditionary Streamers. None.

Decorations. Distinguished Unit Citations: Sicily, [Jun–Jul] 1943; Cassino, 12–14 May 1944; Germany, 24 Mar 1945.

Emblem On a Blue disc, border of nine Golden Orange segments fimbriated of the field, issuing out of sinister chief toward dexter base a Golden Orange winged panther in striking position, proper, between four Yellow stars in dexter chief and five like stars in sinister base. Approved on 24 Jun 1944 (K 2823).

Lineage and Honors History
of the
100ᵗʰ FLYING TRAINING SQUADRON

Lineage. Constituted 100ᵗʰ Pursuit Squadron (Interceptor) on 27 Dec 1941. Activated on 19 Feb 1942. Redesignated: 100ᵗʰ Fighter Squadron on 15 May 1942; 100ᵗʰ Fighter Squadron, Single Engine, on 15 Sep 1944. Inactivated on 19 Oct 1945. Activated on 1 Jul 1947. Inactivated on 1 Jul 1949. Consolidated (19 Sep 1985) with the 100ᵗʰ Air Refueling Squadron, Medium, which was constituted on 8 Jan 1953. Activated on 20 Jan 1953. Inactivated on 25 Nov 1953. Activated on 8 Sep 1954. Discontinued, and inactivated, on 25 Jun 1966. Redesignated: 100ᵗʰ Air Refueling Squadron, Heavy, on 19 Sep 1985; 100ᵗʰ Flying Training Squadron on 29 Aug 1989. Activated on 1 Sep 1989. Inactivated on 1 Apr 1993. Activated in the Reserve on 1 Apr 1999.

Assignments. Southeast Air Corps (later, Army Air Forces) Training Center, 19 Feb 1942; Third Air Force, 4 Jul 1942; 332d Fighter Group, 13 Oct 1942-19 Oct 1945. 332d Fighter Group, 1 Jul 1947-1 Jul 1949. 40ᵗʰ Air Division, 20 Jan 1953; 801ˢᵗ Air Division, 23 May 1953 (attached to 91ˢᵗ Strategic Reconnaissance Wing, 23 May-23 Nov 1953); 40ᵗʰ Air Division, 24-25 Nov 1953. Second Air Force, 8 Sep 1954 (attached to 19ᵗʰ Bombardment Wing, 2 Feb 1955-15 Aug 1956); 100ᵗʰ Bombardment Wing, 16 Aug 1956-25 Jun 1966. 82d Flying Training Wing, 1 Sep 1989; 82d Operations Group, 15 Dec 1991- 1 Apr 1993. 340ᵗʰ Flying Training Group, 1 Apr 1999-.

Stations. Tuskegee AAB, AL, 19 Feb 1942; Selfridge Field, MI, 29 Mar 1943; Oscoda AAFld, MI, 29 Oct 1943; Selfridge Field, MI, 8 Nov-22 Dec 1943; Montecorvino, Italy, 3 Feb 1944; Capodichino, Italy, 21 Feb 1944; Ramitelli, Italy, 6 Jun 1944; Catollica, Italy, c. 4 May 1945; Lucerna, Italy, c. 18 Jul-Sep 1945; Camp Kilmer, NJ, 17-19 Oct 1945. Lockbourne AAB (later AFB), OH, 1 Jul 1947-1 Jul 1949. Turner AFB, GA, 20 Jan 1953; Lockborne AFB, OH, 23 May 1953; Turner AFB, GA, 24-25 Nov 1953.

Robins AFB, GA, 8 Sep 1954; Portsmouth (later, Pease) AFB, NH, 16 Aug 1956-25 Jun 1966. Williams AFB, AZ, 1 Sep 1989-1 Apr 1993. Randolph AFB, TX, 1 Apr 1999-.

Commanders. Unkn, 19 Feb 1942-Jan 1943; Capt James Hunter, 15 Jan 1943; 1Lt Mac Ross, 26 Jan 1943; 1Lt George L. Knox, 5 Apr 1943; 1Lt Elwood T. Driver, 29 Jun 1943; Capt Robert B. Tresville, 6 Jul 1943; Maj Andrew D. Turner, 22 Jun 1944; Capt Roscoe C. Brown, Jun 1945-unkn. Maj Andrew D. Turner, 1 Jul 1947; Capt Elwood T. Driver, c. 15 Aug 1947; Capt Herbert V. Clark, Apr 1948; Capt Joseph D. Elsberry, May 1948; 1Lt Samuel W. Watts, Jr., Jun 1948; Capt Joseph D. Elsberry, 14 Jul 1948; Capt Elwood T. Driver, 30 Sep 1948-1 Jul 1949. None (not manned), 20 Jan-Jun 1953; Maj Clifford E. Cobb, 9 Jul-25 Nov 1953. None (not manned), 8 Sep-19 Oct 1954; Lt Col William E. Smith, 20 Oct 1954; Lt Col Savell L. Sharp, 31 Mar 1956; Lt Col Frank L. Davis, 27 Feb 1958; Maj Harold G. Goodlad, 5 Jan 1959; Lt Col Joseph M. McHale, 29 Jun 1959; Lt Col Glen F. Redmond, 1 Apr 1964; Lt Col John M. Gaither, 1 Mar 1965; Lt Col Jack W. Baker, 25 Oct 1965-unkn (at least through 31 Mar 1966). Lt Col Thomas L. Powell, 1 Sep 1989; Lt Col David M. McIntosh, 27 Aug 1991-1 Apr 1993.

Aircraft. P-39, 1943, 1944; P-40, 1943; P-47, 1944; P-51, 1944-1945. P-47, 1947-1949. KB-29, 1953. KC-97, 1954-1965.

Operations. One of the famous all-black squadrons of the 332d Fighter Group. Combat in MTO and ETO, 19 Feb 1944-26 Apr 1945. Trained in P-47 aircraft, 1947-1949. Air refueling, 1955-1965. Provided academic and upgrade pilot training and managed the Accelerated Copilot Enrichment (ACE) program, 1989-1993.

Service Streamers. World War II American Theater.

Campaign Streamers. World War II: Rome-Arno; Southern France; North Apennines; Po Valley; Normandy; Northern France; Rhineland; Central Europe; Air Combat, EAME.

Armed Forces Expeditionary Streamers. None.

Decorations. Distinguished Unit Citation: Germany, 24 Mar 1945.

Lineage, Assignments, Stations, and Honors through 6 May 1999.

Commanders, Aircraft, and Operations through 1 April 1993.

Supersedes statement prepared on 12 Sep 1989.

Emblem. Approved on 25 Nov 1944.

Prepared by Edward T Russell

Approved by Judy G. Endicott

Lineage and Honors History
of the
301 Fighter Squadron (AFRC)

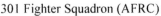

Lineage. Constituted 301 Fighter Squadron on 4 Jul 1942. Activated on 13 Oct 1942. Redesignated 301 Fighter Squadron, Single Engine, c. 21 Aug 1944. Inactivated on 19 Oct 1945. Activated on 1 Jul 1947. Inactivated on 1 Jul 1949. Consolidated (19 Sep 1985) with the 901 Air Refueling Squadron, Heavy, which was constituted on 7 Apr 1958. Activated on 1 Aug 1958. Inactivated on 2 Jul 1969. Redesignated 301 Fighter Squadron on 1 Dec 1999. Activated in the Reserve on 1 Jan 2000.

Assignments. 332 Fighter Group, 13 Oct 1942-19 Oct 1945. 332 Fighter Group, 1 Jul 1947-1 Jul 1949. 4228 Strategic Wing, 1 Aug 1958; 454 Bombardment Wing, 1 Feb 1963-2 Jul 1969 (attached to 4252 Strategic Wing, Dec 1965-Mar 1966 and Jul-Dec 1967). 944 Operations Group, 1 Jan 2000-.

Stations. Tuskegee AAFld, AL, 13 Oct 1942; Selfridge Field, MI, 29 Mar 1943; Oscoda AAFld, MI, 9 Nov 1943; Selfridge Field, MI, 19 Nov 1943-23 Dec 1943; Taranto, Italy, 29 Jan 1944; Montecorvino, Italy, 8 Feb 1944; Capodichino, Italy, 15 Apr 1944; Ramitelli Airdrome, Italy, 30 May 1944; Cattolica Airdrome, Italy, c. 4 May 1945; Lucera Airdrome, Italy, c. 18 Jul-30 Sep 1945; Camp Kilmer, NJ, 17-19 Oct 1945. Lockbourne AAB (later, AFB), OH, 1 Jul 1947-1 Jul 1949. Columbus AFB, MS, 1 Aug 1958-2 Jul 1969. Luke AFB, AZ, 1 Jan 2000-.

Commanders. 1Lt Frederick E. Miles, 15 Jan 1943; Capt Charles H. Debow, 26 Jan 1943; Capt Lee Rayford, 28 Feb 1944; Capt Armour G. McDaniel, Jan 1945; Capt Walter M. Downs, c. 25 Mar 1945-unkn. Capt Charles I. Williams, by 1 Oct 1947; Capt Richard C. Pullam (acting), 30 Apr 1948; Capt Charles I. Williams, Aug 1948; Capt Richard C. Pullam, 25 Aug 1948-30 Apr 1949; unkn, 1 May-1 Jul 1949. Capt Dino Perazzola, c. 1 Aug 1958; Lt Col Homer W. Lear, 22 Oct 1958; Lt Col Malcolm P. Micklewait, c. Aug 1960; Lt Col Everett C. Sunderman, c. Aug 1963; Lt Col Alexander O. Froede, Jr., by Jun 1964; Lt Col Homer B. Wells, by Jun 1965; Lt Col Franklin C. Kendziora, 5 Aug 1966; Lt Col Seth W. Scruggs, by Mar 1968; Lt Col Ralph M. Falkner, by Jun 1968-2 Jul 1969.

Aircraft. P-39, P-40, 1943-1944; P-47, 1944; P-51, 1944-1945. P-47, 1947-1949. KC-135, 1958-1969.

Operations. One of four African-American fighter squadrons to enter combat during World War Two. Combat in ETO and MTO, 15 Feb 1944-26 Apr 1945. Aerial refueling operations under Strategic Air Command, 1959-1969.

Service Streamers. World War II American Theater.

Campaign Streamers. *World War II*: Rome-Arno; Southern France; North Apennines; Po Valley; Normandy; Northern France; Rhineland; Central Europe; Air Combat, EAME Theater.

Armed Forces Expeditionary Streamers. None.

Decorations. Distinguished Unit Citation: Germany, 24 Mar 1945. Air Force Outstanding Unit Awards: 6 Oct 1959-15 Jul 1960; 1-31 Jul 1965 and 1 Dec 1965-1 Mar 1966 [one award]; 2 Mar-1 Apr 1966 and 1 Jul-31 Dec 1967 [one award]; 1 Jul-1 Dec 1968.

Lineage, Assignments, Components, Stations, and Honors through 25 Sep 2000.

Commanders, Aircraft, and Operations through 30 Jun 1969.

Supersedes statement prepared on 2 Apr 1974.

Emblem. Approved on 29 Jun 1945.

Prepared by Forrest L. Marion.

Approved by Judy G. Endicott.

Lineage and Honors History
of the
302 Fighter Squadron (AFRC)

Lineage. Constituted 302 Fighter Squadron on 4 Jul 1942. Activated on 13 Oct 1942. Redesignated 302 Fighter Squadron, Single Engine on 21 Aug 1944. Inactivated on 6 Mar 1945. Consolidated (19 Sep 1985) with the 302 Air Rescue Squadron, which was constituted on 1 Aug 1956. Activated in the Reserve on 8 Oct 1956. Redesignated: 302 Aerospace Rescue and Recovery Squadron on 18 Jan 1966; 302 Special Operations Squadron on 10 Apr 1974; 302 Tactical Fighter Squadron on 1 Jul 1987; 302 Fighter Squadron on 1 Feb 1992.

Assignments. 332 Fighter Group, 13 Oct 1942-6 Mar 1945. 2348 Air Reserve Flying Center, 8 Oct 1956; Fourth Air Force, 24 Jun 1960; Sixth Air Force Reserve Region, 1 Sep 1960; Western Air Force Reserve Region, 31 Dec 1969; Tenth Air Force, 8 Oct 1976; Fourth Air Force, 1 Mar 1983; 944 Tactical Fighter (later, 944 Fighter) Group, 1 Jul 1987; 944 Operations Group, 1 Aug 1992-.

Stations. Tuskegee AAB, AL, 13 Oct 1942; Selfridge Field, MI, 29 Mar 1943; Oscoda AAFld, MI, 19 Nov 1943; Selfridge Field, MI, 1-22 Dec 1943; Taranto, Italy, 1 Feb 1944; Montecorvino, Italy, 7 Feb 1944; Capodichino, Italy, 6 Mar 1944; Ramitelli Afld, Italy, c. 28 May 1944-6 Mar 1945. Williams AFB, AZ, 8 Oct 1956; Luke AFB, AZ, 23 Oct 1960-.

Commanders. None (not manned), 13 Oct 1942-Mar 1943; 2nd Lt William

T. Mattison, 11 Mar 1943; 1ˢᵗ Lt Robert B. Tresville, 29 May 1943; 1ˢᵗ Lt
Edward C. Gleed, 6 Jul 1943; Capt Melvin T. Jackson, 22 Apr 1944; Capt
Vernon V. Haywood, Jan 1945-unkn. Maj Alvin J. Moser Jr., 8 Oct 1956;
Lt Col William D. Hardy, 4 Jan 1960; Maj Cortez C. Brown (additional
duty), 18 Mar 1960; Col Alvin J. Moser Jr., 9 May 1960; Col Victor M
Coale, Dec 1967; Lt Col Henry E. Sherrill, 19 Mar 1971-unkn; Lt Col Paul
B. Heironimus, unkn; Lt Col Amos R. Dreessen, unkn; Lt Col William B.
McDaniel, c. Apr 1973; Lt Col Thomas R. Cooper, 26 Jul 1976; Lt Col Peter
T. Pomonis, 10 Sep 1976; Col Thomas R. Cooper, Sep 1978; Lt Col Bruce
P. Wood, 26 Aug 1980; Col James W. Matchette, 15 May 1981; Col Daniel
L. Blanton, 28 Sep 1983; Maj Paul R. Davis, 27 Aug 1984; Lt Col Jon E.
Hannan, 1 Sep 1985; none (not manned), 1-30 Jun 1987; Lt Col Stephen S.
Summers, by Jan 1988; Lt Col Robert L. Brown, 1 Mar 1991; Lt Col Floyd
C. Williams, 13 Sep 1992; Lt Col Roger A. Binder, 14 Oct 1995; Maj Patrick
J. Shay, 13 Jul 1997-.
Aircraft. P-40, 1943; P-39, 1943-1944; P-47, 1944; P-51, 1944-1945.
SA(later, HU)-16, 1956-1971; HH-34, 1971-1974; CH-3, 1974-1987; HH-
3, 1985-1987; F-16, 1987-.
Operations. One of four African-American fighter squadrons to enter
combat in World War II. Combat in ETO and MTO, 17 Feb 1944-20 Feb
1945. Trained in the Reserve for and performed search and rescue, in addition
to some medical air evacuation missions, mainly in the southwestern United
States, 1956-1974. In 1974, mission changed to training for a combat SAR
role, while continuing to perform some search and rescue. Changed, in mid-
1987, to a fighter role and trained for counterair, interdiction, and close air
support missions. Deployed several times since late 1992 to Turkey to help
enforce the no-fly zone over Iraq and to Italy to support UN air operations
in the Balkans.
Service Streamers. World War II American Theater.
Campaign Streamers. *World War II:* Rome-Arno; Normandy; Northern
France; Southern France; Rhineland; North Apennines; Air Combat, EAME
Theater.
Armed Forces Expeditionary Streamers. None.
Decorations. Air Force Outstanding Unit Awards: 1 Apr 1974-31 Dec
1975; 1 Jul 1987-31 Aug 1989; 1 Jan 1990-31 Dec 1991; 1 Jan 1992-30 Jun
1993; 28 Nov 1993-6 Feb 1994; 6 Sep 1998-5 Sep 2000.
Lineage, Assignments, Stations, and Honors through 30 Aug 2001
Commanders, Aircraft, and Operations through 30 Sep 1998
Supersedes statement prepared on 7 Jan 1986
Emblem. Approved on 2 Nov 1944
Prepared by Judy G. Endicott

Lineage and Honors History
of the
332ⁿᵈ Air Expeditionary Group (ACC)

Lineage. Established as 332ⁿᵈ Fighter Group on 4 Jul 1942. Activated on 13 Oct 1942. Inactivated on 19 Oct 1945. Activated on 1 Jul 1947. Inactivated on 1 Jul 1949. Redesignated 332ⁿᵈ Air Expeditionary Group, and converted to provisional status, on 19 Nov 1998. Activated on 1 Dec 1998.

Assignments. Third Air Force, 13 Oct 1942; First Air Force, 23 Jul 1943; Twelfth Air Force, c. 27 Jan 1944; XII Air Force Training and Replacement Command (Provisional), 3 Feb 1944; XII Fighter Command, 10 Feb 1944; 62ⁿᵈ Fighter Wing, 10 Feb 1944; Fifteenth Air Force, 22 May 1944; 306ᵗʰ Fighter Wing, 22 May 1944; 305ᵗʰ Bombardment Wing, 12 Jun-Sep 1945; unkn, Sep-19 Oct 1945. Ninth Air Force, 1 Jul 1947; 332ⁿᵈ Fighter Wing, 15 Aug 1947-1 Jul 1949. 9ᵗʰ Air and Space Expeditionary Task Force-Southern Watch, 1 Dec 1998-.

Components. *Squadrons.* **9ᵗʰ** Expeditionary Fighter: 16-28 Dec 1998. **18ᵗʰ** Expeditionary Fighter: 1 Dec 1998-2 Mar 1999. **34ᵗʰ** Expeditionary Fighter: 1 Dec 1998-2 Mar 1999. **55ᵗʰ** Expeditionary Fighter: 19 Jan-4 May 1999. **68ᵗʰ** Expeditionary Fighter: 3 Mar-23 Apr 1999. **69ᵗʰ** Expeditionary Fighter: 23 Apr-1 Oct 1999. **70ᵗʰ** Expeditionary Fighter: 4 May-1 Oct 1999. **99ᵗʰ** Fighter: 1 May 1944-22 Jun 1945 (detached 1 May-6 Jun and 11-30 Jun 1944); 1 Jul 1947-1 Jul 1949. **100ᵗʰ** Fighter: 13 Oct 1942-19 Oct 1945; 1 Jul 1947-1 Jul 1949. **301ˢᵗ** Fighter: 13 Oct 1942-19 Oct 1945; 1 Jul 1947-1 Jul 1949. **302ⁿᵈ** Fighter: 13 Oct 1942-6 Mar 1945. **332ⁿᵈ** Expeditionary Rescue: 1 Dec 1998-. **355ᵗʰ** Expeditionary Fighter: 1-21 Dec 1998. **391ˢᵗ** Expeditionary Fighter: 19 Jan-9 Mar 1999. **522ⁿᵈ** Expeditionary Fighter: 15 Dec 1998-8 Feb 1999.

Stations. Tuskegee, AL, 13 Oct 1942; Selfridge Field, MI, 29 Mar 1943; Oscoda, MI, 12 Apr 1943; Selfridge Field, MI, 9 Jul-22 Dec 1943; Montecorvino, Italy, 8 Feb 1944; Capodichino, Italy, 15 Apr 1944; Ramitelli Airfield, Italy, 28 May 1944; Cattolica, Italy, c. 4 May 1945; Lucera, Italy, c. 18 Jul-Sep 1945; Camp Kilmer, NJ, 17-19 Oct 1945. Lockbourne AAB (later, AFB), OH, 1 Jul 1947-1 Jul 1949. Al Jaber, Kuwait, 1 Dec 1998-.

Commanders. Lt Col Sam W. Westbrook, Jr., by 19 Oct 1942; Col Robert R. Selway, Jr., 16 May 1943; Col Benjamin O. Davis, Jr., 8 Oct 1943; Maj George S. Roberts, 3 Nov 1944; Col Benjamin O. Davis, Jr., 24 Dec 1944; Maj George S. Roberts, 9 Jun 1945-unkn. Unkn, 1 Jul-27 Aug 1947; Maj William A. Campbell, 28 Aug 1947-1 Jul 1949.

Aircraft. P-40, 1943-1944; P-39, 1943-1944; P-47, 1944; P-51, 1944-1945. P(later F)-47, 1947-1949.

Operations. Only all-African-American fighter group in World War II, also known informerly as "The Tuskegee Airman." Trained for combat at Tuskegee, Alabama and bases in Michigan with P-39 and P-40 aircraft. Moved to Italy, January-early February 1944. Began combat with Twelfth Air Force on 5 February. Used P-39s to escort convoys, protect harbors, and fly armed reconnaissance missions. Converted to P-47s during April-May 1944 and to P-51s in June. Operated with Fifteenth Air Force from May 1944 to April 1945, being engaged primarily in protecting bombers that struck such objectives as oil refineries, factories, airfields, and marshalling yards in Italy, France, Germany, Poland, Czechoslovakia, Austria, Hungary, Yugoslavia, Rumania, Bulgaria, and Greece. Also made strafing attacks on airdromes, railroads, highways, bridges, river traffic, troop concentrations, radar facilities, power stations, and other targets. Received a DUC for a mission on 24 March 1945 when the group escorted B-17s during a raid on a tank factory at Berlin, fought the interceptors that attacked the formation, and strafed transportation facilities while flying back to the base in Italy. Returned to the U.S. in October and inactivated on 19 Oct 1945. Activated again in July 1947 as a part of Tactical Air Command (TAC). Trained with P(later F)-47s, ferried aircraft, and took part in TAC exercises. Inactivated two years later on 1 July 1949.

Service Streamers. World War II American Theater.

Campaign Streamers. *World War II:* Rome-Arno; Normandy; Northern France; Southern France; North Apennines; Rhineland; Central Europe; Po Valley; Air Combat, EAME Theater.

Armed Forces Expeditionary Streamers. None.

Decorations. Distinguished Unit Citation: Germany, 24 Mar 1945.

Lineage, Assignments, Components, Stations, and Honors through 6 Dec 1999

Commanders, Aircraft, and Operations through 1 Jul 1949

Supersedes published information contained in Maurer Maurer (ed.), *Air Force Combat Units of World War II* (Washington: USGPO, 1983).

Emblem. Approved on 15 Jan 1943

Prepared by Judy G. Endicott

1067263003: CLASS 42-E
P4068 -- (G-327-722G-318AB) (9-11-42-1P) (12"-0) (CLASS 42-E) Order Unknown -- James B. Knighton, George L. Knox, Lee Rayford, Sherman W. White.

1067263001: CLASS 42-C, MEMBERS OF THE FIRST GRADUATING CLASS
P4066 -- Left to Right: Captain B. O. Davis, Jr., 2nd Lt. Lemuel R. Curtis, 2nd Lt. George S. Roberts, 2nd Lt. Charles Debow, 2nd Lt. Mac Ross.

1067263002: CLASS 42-D
P4067 – (G-329-722G-318AB) (9-11-42-1P) (12"-0) (CLASS 42-D) Order Unknown – Sidney P. Brooks, Charles W. Dryden, Clarence C. Jamison.

1067263008: CLASS 42-I
P4073 – Left to Right: Nathaniel M. Hill, Marshall S. Cabiness, Herman A. Lawson, William T. Mattison, John A. Gibson, Elwood T. Driver, Price D. Rice, Andrew D. Turner.

1067263009: CLASS 42-J
P4074 – Left to Right: Jerome T. Edwards, Terry J. Charlton, Howard L. Baugh, Melvin T. Jackson.

1067263007: CLASS 42-H
P4072 – (G-440-722G-318AB) (9-1-42-9A) (6 3/8-0) Left to Right: Front Row – Samuel M. Bruce,
Wilmore B. Leonard, James L. McCullin, Henry Perry. Back Row – John H. Morgan, Richard C. Caesar,
Edward L. Toppins, Robert W. Deiz, Joseph D. Elsberry.

1067263010: CLASS 42-K
P4075 -- Order Unknown: Edward C. Gleed, Milton T. Hall, Wendell O. Pruitt, Richard C. Pullam, Peter
C. Verwayne, William H. Walker, Romeo M. Williams, Robert B. Tresville, Jr.

1067263006: CLASS 42-G
P4071 -- (G356-722G-318AB) (8-1-42-10A)(6 3/8-0) Order Unknown -- Richard Davis, Willie Fuller,
Cassius Harris, Earl E. King, Walter E. Lawson, John H. McClure, Leon C. Roberts, John W. Roberts.

CPSIA information can be obtained at www.ICGtesting.com
Printed in the USA
BVOW03s1407161114

375307BV00001B/57/A